Lou Singletary-Bedford

Driftwood - Driftings

Lou Singletary-Bedford

Driftwood - Driftings

ISBN/EAN: 9783744643283

Printed in Europe, USA, Canada, Australia, Japan

Cover: Foto ©Andreas Hilbeck / pixelio.de

More available books at **www.hansebooks.com**

DRIFTWOOD,

BY

MRS. LOU SINGLETARY-BEDFORD,

AND

DRIFTINGS,

BY

MRS. MAY BEDFORD-EAGAN.

———

DALLAS:
A. D. ALDRIDGE & CO.
1893.

INSCRIPTION.

To all those whose heart and hand are in sympathy with the work of encouraging and developing the genius and talent of our own beautiful Southland, in every department of literature, and to the memory of the beloved daughter whose name is associated with hers in this publication, but whose early death dissipated the hopes and aspirations of years, and cut short a life that promised to be useful, this little volume is respectfully and affectionately inscribed by THE AUTHOR.

BIOGRAPHICAL.

Mrs. Lou Singletary-Bedford is the fifth child and third daughter of Luther and Elizabeth Stell-Singletary. Her father, descended from an old and honored English family, was born in Grafton, Mass., in October, 1796. Receiving a finished education in Boston, he emigrated to Petersburg, Va., where he was for a time engaged as professor of music and literature. At this place he married a Mrs. Morgan, an accomplished and beautiful young widow.

Seized with a desire to press on towards the great West, and to unite his fortunes with its own, Mr. Singletary and his wife soon removed to Middle Tennessee, and from that State finally went to Kentucky, where, in the village of Feliciana, Mrs. Bedford was born and passed the early years of her life.

Inheriting the refined tastes and sensibilities of both father and mother, she soon developed a rare talent for literature, which only freed itself by breathing out its spirit in verses that even then were remarkable for that soft melody and grace which have since characterized her work.

The warm sympathetic nature of the child was intensified and quickened into poesy by the natural beauty and gentle peace of her surroundings, and her earliest published poems were well received. One of her sweetest and most popular poems, "My Childhood's Home," was written in her fifteenth year. In a revised and more extended form it appears in her first collection of poems.

Adopting the pen name of "Lenora" she contributed to periodicals work that won the highest commendation, and decided her to renewed efforts in the field of literature.

While yet a girl she became a teacher in the schools of her vicinity, in which occupation she continued until her marriage, in 1857, to John Joseph Bedford, a descendent of Gunning Bedford, one of the signers of the Constitution of the United States. Being a man of refined tastes and acknowledged talent he was a fit husband for his gifted wife.

In the financial panic of 1857 her husband's fortunes were so much impaired that, busied with the duties of wife and mother and oppressed with life's cares, the pen was laid aside not to be taken up again till the storm of war ceased and the sunshine of peace and prosperity shone through the lifting clouds.

In 1878 she accompanied her husband to Florida, where he went in the interest of his health. In Milton, in that State, he took charge of the *"Standard"* to which Mrs. Bedford contributed with so much success that she was induced to drop her *nom de plume* and write over her own name.

In the year 1881, while still residing in Florida, her first collection of poems, "A Vision and Other Poems," was brought out by the publishing house of Robert Clark & Company, Cincinnati. A London publisher visiting Florida saw a copy of the work and secured permission to reproduce it in England, and accordingly issued it a few months subsequently.

This volume received the most flattering recognition. It was at once recognized to be the work of a poet. Paul H. Hayne spoke warmly in its favor. Oliver Wendell Holmes, writing to Mrs. Bedford, after a review of the poems, says: "I recognize in your poems a sincere human feeling—a character which always commends any poetical effort." Longfellow, amid the praise of the world found time to write a letter of encouragement and well-wishes, and a host of others, able critics and authors, were not insensible to the merits of the work.

The Louisville *Courier-Journal*, to which Mrs. Bedford was at one time a frequent contributor, speaking of this work, says: "Mrs. Lou S. Bedford is compared by many to Felicia Hemans; and permit me to suggest that her name be inscribed as high upon the scroll of honor and worth as that of Paul H. Hayne. There is the sweet charm of dignity, decorum and morality; yea, even more, of Christianity, breathing from her lines. There are beauty and variety, as she paints from some image before her mental eye; and truth, as she blends some internal passion of noble thought with the most beautiful imagery and choicest language. Like Mrs. Hemans, a tone of unforced, persuasive goodness, pervades her poetry; and though often sad, it is never complaining. That she is a great-hearted, womanly woman, to whose ear the words, home, husband, children and friends, are terms of sweetest import, no one can doubt who is fortunate enough to possess a copy of her elegant poems, called 'A Vision and Other Poems.' The Vision is a tribute to the North for her magnanimity and beautiful charity to the South in 1878, when the yellow fever had desolated and depopulated so many cities and homes. The outpourings of a mighty sympathy dictated this poem; while the fragrant incense of a nation's gratitude breathes and burns through the inspiration of this woman's pen. And well may we be proud of and rejoice in her success; for, although classed among the Southern poets, 'this star-eyed, night-haired' queen of Southern song is a native of our own grand old Kentucky; and only a few years ago sought a home beneath sunnier skies."

For the past several years Mrs. Bedford has resided in Dallas, Texas, where some of her best work has been done. The collection, "Gathered Leaves," her last published volume, has been deservedly popular, and has won for her most sincere admirers wherever it has been read.   A——.

'I soar—I'm drawn up like the lark
To its white cloud: So high my mark,
Albeit my wing is small and dark.

   * * *

'I only would have leave to loose,
(In tears and blood, if so He choose)
Mine inward music out to use.

   * * *

'Only embrace and be embraced
By fiery ends—whereby to waste
And light God's future with my past.

      —E. B. BROWNING.

PREFACE.

It is said that prefaces are out of date; nevertheless, I am sufficiently old-fashioned to believe that a word of explanation is often necessary to bring the reader and writer into sympathy with each other.

Heretofore I have confined my publications to poetry; but in this miscellaneous collection I have interspersed prose with recently written poems, together with others not embraced in the former volumes. I have also gathered together the short stories and other literary remains of my daughter, Mrs. May Bedford-Eagan, and included them in this work. Had not death intervened she intended publishing these under the title here used—Driftings. In that event mine would have been called Miscellaneous Pencilings—a title under which I have contributed much to the press. I have chosen Driftwood and Driftings as being a more euphoneous combination than the other names would have been. Doubtless her work would have been more finished had she lived to revise it; but to me it is sacred as it is—I have made few changes.

In regard to "Maude Arnold" I would say that the characters are not a creation of the brain alone. The father and daughter are real actors, though imagination has played a part sometimes in their surroundings. Its beauty, however, is not in the romance itself, but in the gradual unfolding of mind and character, together with the life-like blending of the religious, the skeptical and the philosophical train of thought as committed to her diary by the heroine. I do not think the original plan of the story was fulfilled—the abrupt termination was the result of circumstances, the writer marrying about a week after the last installment was sent to the press.

• It is a sad pleasure to have my name connected in this way with one so dear—with one whose life was an exponent of the religion she professed, and whose writings are an exponent of the life she lived.

DALLAS, TEXAS, Feb. 9, 1893.   L. S. B.

CONTENTS.

DRIFTWOOD.

THE WORLD'S PROGRESS.

" There is no standing still !   Even as we pause
   The steep path shifts and we slip back a pace ;
Movement is safety ; by the journey's laws
   No help is given, no safe abiding place ;
No idling in the pathway, hard and slow ;
We must go backward or must forward go.

"Ah, blessed law ! for rest is passing sweet,
   And we would all lie down if so we might ;
And few would struggle on with bleeding feet,
   And few would ever gain the higher height ;
Except for the stern law that makes us know
We must go forward, or must backward go."

At this age of the world there is no such thing
as standing still.   The Star of Empire has risen upon
the western hemisphere, and its light is penetrating
every section of this great country, while the same

vitality that has given yankeedom its character for
enterprise is permeating our sluggish veins, and with
the spirit of the Nineteenth Century upon us, we, too,
are moving onward. Should we attempt to pause we
should be swept aside by the irresistible wheels of
Progress, whose marks are visible on every side, and
whose motions cannot be stopped. They may be
checked, but only for a time, that they may gain
leverage for a more vigorous onset. They are destined
to override every obstacle to the attainment of their
appointed end. The silent forces of Nature are constantly at work developing the wonders of the vegetable, the animal, and the mineral kingdoms; and
the no less silent forces of mind are developing results
the mentioning of which one hundred years ago
would have startled the most learned sage. But
step by step, revolution by revolution, these wheels
have rolled on, until wonder is a scarcely remembered
emotion.

The spirit of Progress, at first slow, has gained
strength by the way. She has brought Science to her
aid—or, rather, she is the offspring of Science, whose
birth has no date in Time's calendar, but whose rivulets, one by one, have united, until now, with channel
widened and deepened, the current flows on toward a

vast sea, whose depths cannot be fathomed. Through
her assistance see what steam has accomplished:

Could Fulton, when he launched his first rude boat,
  Have viewed the nations with prophetic eye,
And seen the stately vessels now afloat,
  And the long line of steam cars rushing by,
How the grand vision of the power of steam
Would have surpassed even his wildest dream.

And who would have thought that the discovery
of the identity of lightning with electricity would
result in such wonderful developments? Truly,

When Franklin caught the lightning in his grasp—
  Drew the electric current from its place—
None dreamed he forged the link by which to clasp
  The sundered nations in a close embrace;
But now, swifter than wind, with magic bound,
From clime to clime Thought sweeps the world around.

Thus we see that from one small link has grown a
great chain of electric inventions and discoveries, including the telegraph, cable, electric light and electric
railway, and the thoughtful mind sees others in dim
perspective. Verily, the end is not yet.

And when, in 1819, George Stevenson constructed
his first locomotive, and in 1821 engineered the railway between Liverpool and Manchester, over which

locomotives were to pass at the rate of twelve miles an hour, little did he imagine that in less than half a century railroads, constructed on this plan, overleaping all barriers, bridging rivers and bays, leveling hills, passing underground and penetrating mountains, would form a network throughout the civilized world, over which the iron steed would travel at the rate of sixty or seventy miles an hour. But time would fail us should we attempt to follow the signs of advancement to be seen around us. Industry in her various forms is lending her aid to Science, and heaven, by its smiles and tears, its clouds and its sunshine, is constantly contributing to the world's prosperity; and the eminence we have at present attained is but an earnest of what the future holds in store for those who "labor and wait."

And now, I would ask, toward what does all this tend? Is it designed by the Allwise alone for man's temporal good, or is there a moral to the picture? Cannot the Christian of this enlightened age see something in the "signs of the times" that is "holden" from other eyes? Does he not perceive the watchful care of the loving Father, as, by means of these scientific inventions, year by year Christianity moves forward on her appointed mission?

The hydra-headed monster, Infidelity, discerns these signs, and, alarmed, is arraying herself for the conflict. Anti-Bible societies are being formed in some of the northern cities, in which the members are not permitted to make any quotation from the sacred pages; if through inadvertence they do so, an apology is required. And even in our own fair city of Dallas, a society has just been formed (1886) called the Secular Union of Freethinkers, the object of which seems to be to so far befog the mind of the unlearned inquirer after truth that he will not be able to perceive the true light. There is this startling statement made by Dr. McKay, the champion of this society—an assertion which the merest tyro in history ought to be able to refute:

"If we had knuckled down to the dictates of the Christian religion we would have had no railroads, no telegraph lines, no steamboats. If it were not for the parties going contrary to those dictates America would never have been discovered."

History has led me to believe that Columbus was a true Christian, in support of which proposition it states that his first act on landing on this continent was that of thanking God for thus crowning with success this great enterprise, which was born of faith.

And when Morse's invention was demonstrated to be
a success, the first message flashed along the wire was:
"See what God hath wrought!" And so conscious
was he that he was moved by an inspiration beyond
himself that when congratulated on his success he
invariably disclaimed all credit, saying that he was
simply an instrument in God's hands in accomplishing this important work. And we ourselves behold
how it is accomplishing that whereunto it was sent,
in that it is being used in transmitting the sermons of
the ambassadors of His court from city to city and
from continent to continent. Other important inventions might be cited bearing in this direction; but it
is sufficient to state that all the great inventions that
have proved to be a blessing to mankind have been
in Christian lands, and have, for the most part, been
the outgrowth of Christian minds.

But is Christianity alarmed? Is the disciple of
the Crucified One startled at these demonstrations on
the part of the infidel world? Far from it. It is
but an evidence that the votaries of infidelity are fear-
ing for their strongholds. When the prince of the
powers of darkness begins to marshal his hosts for an
assault on his Bible and his religion, the Christian
sees in it simply a fulfillment of that which is "writ-

ten," and feels that he is standing on the threshold of a bright epoch in the history of the church.

Freethinking, like other forms of infidelity, is simply a "refuge of lies," behind which thousands hide themselves in their "day of visitation," and from which they are destined to go down to that Plutonian region—

"In whose arm and brain his own redemption lies,"

and from which he will be awakened to a consciousness of his error too late:

> And of all ever written or spoken
>   Too late is the saddest word
> That e'er with its mournful import
>   The innermost spirit stirred.
> 'Tis the knell of a hope that's vanished,
>   The wail of a vain regret,
> The lowest depths of whose anguish
>   Have never been fathomed yet.

Ah! truly, freethinking, notwithstanding the metaphysical glamor thrown around it by Dr. McKay, is but foolishness to one who "spiritually discerns" his immortality; for the wisdom of man, outside of Revelation, only reaches the mind, while the teachings of the word of God take hold on the heart.

And the Author, not content with this Book as an expression of His love, calls and sends ministers to deliver its message. Still not satisfied, He raises up men of genius, whose inventions and discoveries, such as the printing press, railroad, cable and telegraph, notwithstanding Dr. McKay's opinion to the contrary, are intended to facilitate the work of His ambassadors in carrying the gospel to all nations. Verily the goal toward which the spirit of progress is tending throughout the world is the accomplishing of Christ's commission to His disciples—the preaching of the gospel to every creature. Yea,

When for God's glory man would penetrate
    The ice-bound region round the northern pole,
Methinks no obstacle will be too great
    Before the gospel car to backward roll;
Since Science and the Gospel hold the key
Of every door to every land and sea.

And though a myriad perish by the way,
    The work of these twin sisters will go on;
Benighted lands shall see the gospel day,
    Alike 'mid Arctic snows, 'neath tropic sun;
The banner of the Cross remain unfurled,
While it stands written, "INTO ALL THE WORLD."

MY "TEXAS GARLAND."

A dainty garland I have wreathed
  Of flowers from a Texas plain—
All glorious with such radiant hues
  As I may never see again;
For Time has dimmed the rosy light
That made their dewy petals bright.

One, fair and fragile as the vine
  That to the oak doth lightly cling,
Put forth a deeper, lovelier bloom,
  With each recurrence of the spring;
Till Texas prairie never knew
A blossom of a sweeter hue.

On silent wings three years went by,
  And then another tiny bloom
Burst into beauty, and the air
  Was redolent with the perfume;
'Mid lilies set, its starry eyes
Rivaled the azure of the skies.

Then came another tender bud,
  As lovely, but of deeper dye;

As if Italian airs had kissed
  Its rosy leaves in passing by;
Lightly caressed by sun and dew,
Stronger and ruddier it grew.

Uprooting these from native soil,
  We bore afar each precious gem;
But God stooped down and plucked the first,
  And left us but the broken stem,
Which reverently we laid away
To 'wait the Resurrection day.

Exotic, three, on Texas soil,
  Later, took root, and, side by side,
Flourished, till on a winter's day
  One withered, and—'twas said, it died;
But well I know, past earthly ill,
In Heaven it is blooming still.

And then two buds, tender and sweet,
  To comfort my lone heart were given;
Each promising as fair a flower
  As ever burst to bloom in Heaven;
But, needing one to grace His throne,
God took it, leaving us but one.

Of the eight precious blossoms, three
   No longer gladden earthly bowers;
And life holds nothing that can fill
   The void made by my "missing flowérs;"
The others, deeper, stronger, set
In Texas soil, are blooming yet.

Thus one by one each cherished bloom
   Is falling from its earthly stem ;
Those that remain full well I know,
   Will fade and pass away like them,
To form, I trust, in Eden's bower, ·
A "Texas garland" in full flower.

AMERICAN LITERATURE.

The literature of a nation is its most lasting monument. Rivers change their channel, mountains their base. The grand old Mississippi is a worthy illustration of the first statement, some of the most valuable portions of a number of the cities and villages along its banks having fallen in, a corresponding building up or embanking of the sand and soil on the opposite side following as the result; and to-day pleasure boats and vessels of commerce, on the smooth bosom of its waters, glide all unheeding over the submerged land and houses. · For proof of the latter, read the statements of historians and travelers. They tell us that the Heliopolis obelisk, of Egypt, which once stood on an eminence, now has its base several feet below the surrounding plain, the ebb and flow of the great Nile having undermined it. Let this suffice as examples.

Sculptured marble and stone, crumbling beneath the finger of Time, lose their symmetry and their beauty; and it remains for the historian and the poet to transmit in living colors to unborn generations the story of their grandeur and their glory. Recent travelers in Italy tell us that the glory has departed from the Colliseum of the Seven-Hill-City—that grand amphitheatre of Vespasian at Rome. The magnificent temples of Greece, the Parthenon at Athens and the Pantheon, though well-preserved, have not escaped the impress of the centuries. But the pens of the historians of Egypt, of Virgil and Dante, and Herodotus, have raised for their respective countries monuments whose inscriptions will be read with pleasure and profit when those of stone shall have been razed to

the ground, it may be to give place to a later civilization. As an evidence of the imperishable nature of
literature, take that of the Arabian Cushites, who, for
ages, were leaders in civilizing the nations. Of this
fact there are indelible and indisputable records.
They were the first to use weights and measures; and.
long before the Egyptians, who boast of their ancient
civilization, had thought of such a currency, they
used stamped metallic coins; and those who have
seen them say that modern times have not produced
any more beautiful. (Parenthetically let me say here
that it is evident Wisdom was not born with us.)

The earliest of the Cushite Arabian writings that
have come to us were found on a crumbling monument on the coast of Arabia, and deciphered by Rev.
C. Foster, of England. The writing was in three
parts, all relating to the "destruction of an Arabian
war-party named Ac, by the tribe of Ad, a great
grandson of Noah, whose territory the former had,
unprovoked, invaded. In the description of the surroundings the record says: " We walked with slow,
proud step, in needle-worked, many-colored vestments,
in whole-silk, in grass-green checkered robes." It
further states that their Kings recorded: "Good
judgments written in books to be kept; and we pro-

claimed our belief in miracles, in the resurrection and the return into the nostrils of the breath of life." The engraving was made in the Aditic and Hamyritic alphabet, fac-similes of which are given in Mr. Foster's great work on Arabia, and he thinks that the engraving was not made later than five hundred years after the flood. These specimens of pre-historic literature have been rescued by the faithful antiquary, and when the stone, already mouldering, on which they were engraven, shall be buried by some convulsion of nature, or trampled under foot and forgotten, they will stand as living witnesses of the faith and skill of that people.

Let us draw a contrast between the strength of marble and of mind. The pyramid of Cheops, one of the seven wonders of the world, covering an area of more than thirteen acres of ground, and containing material sufficient to build a city as large as our National Capitol, has, for ages, stood as a wonder of art, of architecture and of science. It took four hundred thousand men twenty years to build it; but it has not escaped the ravages of time—the outer masonry is fast mouldering away. From this grand work turn to Homer, the blind minstrel of Smyrna, who lived and sang while the language of his country was yet in its infancy, and when its ballads had not aspired to the dignity of being classed as refined poetry. Macauley says it is probable that Homer never knew a letter; but such a supposition seems unworthy of credence. Long before his time, Cadmus, a son of the King of the Phenicians, who were at that time, the most highly civilized nation on the globe, had furnished sixteen letters to the Greek alphabet, then in its formative state; and in Homer's time the Ionic or Eolic dialect, in which he wrote, was in its highest state of development. Besides, while I would yield due deference to Lord Macauley's opinion, standing as he does at the head of English historians, it certainly seems preposterous to suppose that a man ignorant of letters and their use could attain such perfection of style and purity of diction as are evinced in his renowned poems, the "Iliad" and "Odyssey." And not the least wonder in connection with his work is that it was accomplished without the aid of any of the modern accessories to writing, such as pen, ink and paper, which are esteemed indispensable to a literary career; and when the printing press had not entered into man's dreams. How little did he think the time in which he lived would, through the centuries, be called the Homeric age; or that, translated, his works would be read by every nation of the earth; or that the names of such poets as Dante and Virgil, and even Milton, would borrow luster from the reflected light of his genius! The work of the four hundred thousand men for twenty years is slowly yielding to the influence of time, while this one man, living in an obscure age and laboring under untold disadvantages, has reared a monument to his name and the glory of his country as lasting as time, even though it should stretch away into an infinity of years.

But it was to our own literature, however much I may have digressed, that I esayed to pay my respects in commencing this paper. It has been deridingly said that America—the youngest and fairest of the nations—has no literature. In the sense that she has no distinct or original language, the statement is correct; and this circumstance has, perhaps, prevented her taking as high rank in the world of letters as she otherwise would have done, since in the process of translation into other tongues there is danger of hers passing for English work. She has, however, a distinct literature by reason of her individuality of history, of scenery and of government. The corner-stone in this structure was laid October 28, 1736, when

£400 was voted by the general court of Boston toward a school or college, to which amount, two years later, the learned English clergyman, John Harvard, added £800 and 320 volumes. Thus was commenced Harvard College at Cambridge, Massachusetts, which to-day has, besides landed property, $1,000,000 of invested capital; and around this venerable institution and its "co-laborers, William and Mary, and, later, Princeton and Columbia and Georgetown," cluster the names and works that have created American Literature.

Unlike almost every other nation that has attained any eminence in letters, America has had no dark age in her literature, its foundation having been laid at a time when the English language, having passed through the crucial test of formation, had attained a high degree of purity; and having as its supporters such names as Jonathan Edwards, John Winthrop, Ezra Stiles, Alexander Hamilton, and Benjamin Franklin, who, someone has graphically said, "tore the lightning from heaven, the sceptre from tyrants, and left to American Literature the wisdom of an honest and a great mind."

But in tracing its development, we must admit there was a time when the circumstances which led to the settlement of this great continent gave coloring to all literary production; and not until the fires of religious persecution were extinguished did the intellectual forces come into full action, literature take a wider range in the great field of Thought, and a brighter day dawn in the Empire of Mind. But it is impossible to enumerate the names of all who have contributed to the erection of this imposing structure. The heavens are studded with unnumbered stars, each one yielding its complement of the light that falls in a halo of glory around us, but it is only the few that we can call by name; and so in the great galaxy of the mental Universe, it is only a small number whose writings have formed a pronounced feature of our literature.

When the unrest incident to the Revolution had given place to tranquillity, the magic wand of Poesy was passed over our new and beautiful land, the inspiration of Song came upon our sons and daughters, and through all the years of our nationality the sweetest melodies have kept time to the march of Progress. Year by year has added beauty and richness to American Song, much of which will perhaps prove ephemeral, but the lessons given will doubtless do good in their generation. Indeed, it is pleasant to believe that the meteor-like flashes of light that sweep across the intellectual horizon, fade away and are seemingly lost, instead, often light up some dark mind, and penetrate the clouds gathered about some sorrowing heart.

Nor have the sons of Story been idle. By means of their genius Romance has thrown over our majestic mountains, green valleys, broad rivers and unrivaled lakes and waterfalls, the veiled luster of its drapery, and grove and prairie have become peopled with a race of beings which to the inhabitants of the Old World seem almost as mythical as the fabulous race of the Lilliputians. The pen of James Fenimore Cooper has indeed immortalized our woods, lakes and prairies; woven around the dusky Sons of the Forest a beautiful web of romance which cannot be easily torn away, and opened a new era in the realm of Fiction. The genius of Walter Scott has wreathed with garlands of unfading glory the historic lands of England, Scotland and Wales, laid bare the secrets of Kings and of courts, while Cooper, with equal skill and in a strikingly similar style, has thrown a charm around our forests which the coming years will not weaken; for his pen-pictures are destined to take a permanent place in American literature. The high-

renown of his works is not confined to our own coun·
try. The fisherman of Norway, the merchant of Bor-
deaux, and the scholar of Frankfort, have hung with
delight over his stories of the sea and the thrilling
adventures of the New World, which were at once
translated into their respective languages. This is certainly no small or unworthy tribute to his genius.
Delicacy of thought and refinement of expression
characterize his writings throughout. And if the
mind sometimes becomes weary with the tediousness
of the narrative, it is not for want of gems of thought
along the way, but from impatience to follow the
fortunes of the characters who never fail to interest.
For beauty, tenderness and pathos, some of his scenes
stand pre-eminent and alone. Indeed, I can recall no
picture from the pen of any writer that is at all com-
parable in delicacy of delineation and thrilling interest
to the death scene of Leather Stocking. The silence
that reigned in the camp, the taciturnity of the
Indians, the delicacy of feeling that moved these un-
tutored children of the woods to stuff the skin of his
dog and keep it near the old man, whose senses were
blunted by age, that he might not know that the
companion of his life was gone; their gravity and
their sympathy for him; his springing to his feet just

before breathing his last and exclaiming "Here!" seemingly in answer to the roll call of Heaven, is all portrayed in a masterly manner, that has rarely been equaled, and perhaps never surpassed by a writer of any age.

In the enthusiasm awakened by my admiration of the great pioneer of American Romance, I have to some extent unwittingly anticipated the progress of American literature; but would make amends by returning and taking up the thread of the subject at the point of divergence.

In planning the erection of a building designed to withstand the ravages of time, too much pains can scarcely be taken in giving it a secure foundation; lest in the coming years it should fall and become simply a mass of mouldering ruins. The same is true in regard to the construction of a language or a litera- ture. In accordance with reason and the universal fitness of things, it is impossible for a Nation com- posed of different nationalities and tongues to build for itself a distinctive name and character in the great world of letters without laying the foundation of such a structure. This thought was early impressed upon the minds of the educators of America as a result of their observance of a "vicious pronunciation which

prevailed extensively among the common people,"
notwithstanding the formative period of the prevailing
language extended backward through centuries; and,
while yet the subsiding thunders of the Revolution
were reverberating among the New England hills, and
the infant voice of Freedom rejoicing over the broken
bonds of Tyranny and the birth of a Nation, the
dream of emancipating the English tongue from the
tyrant, Ignorance, into whose hands it had fallen,
dawned upon the mind of Noah Webster; and he at
once set about the work of preparing the chief corner
stone destined to become the support of the grandest
and most universally spoken language in the world.

However, before attempting to trace the development of a work of such magnitude aud far-reaching
importance it will not be out of place to give a condensed sketch of the lineage, and life of its author.
Noah Webster, the son of a highly respectable farmer
of Connecticut, was born in Hartford on the 16th of
October, 1758. He was a descendant in the fourth
generation of John Webster, an early settler of that
city, and at one time Governor of Connecticut. On
the maternal side he was a descendant of William
Bradford, the second Governor of Plymouth Colony;
and thus it appears that the tides that met in the

future lexicographer's veins were Pilgrim and Puritan, without dilution from less sterling sources. It is seen by this that he was of fine lineage on both sides, since in that day merit was more generally the basis on which men were chosen than now, when political preferment is, alas, too often the result of a corrupt ballot, and not the expression of the unbiased wishes of the people.

As in the case of most great men of America, Poverty was the ungentle and austere disciplinarian that guided him amid dark labyrinths and intricate passages, until, a well-developed illustration of her wholesome tutelage, he came forth prepared for the long and tedious research necessary for the work of his life. In him is presented a fair illustration of the true proposition that Nature is not blind in her gifts —since his inherent tastes were so perfectly suited to the scion of a family for generations distinguished for longevity, several of his immediate ancestors having attained the remarkable age of eighty or ninety years. Indeed, a work of such vast compass could not, from its incipiency, reach completion in the course of an ordinary lifetime.

The difficulties which Mr. Webster experienced in establishing himself in business after completing his course at Yale, where he graduated with honor in 1778, will better be appreciated when it is remembered that the war of Independence, with all its sorrowful details of trials and hardships, was devastating the colonies, and that the final result was afar off and uncertain. But with the dauntless courage that characterized him throughout a long and busy and useful life, he left his home to carve out his own fortune, with only $4.00 of our present currency in his purse—the parting gift of his father. His first essay in this direction was teaching school in his native city, Hartford. He also commenced the study of law; the resort then, as printing is now, of young men whose aspirations point them to something more congenial to the intellectual nature than is manual labor. Verily, the law and the printer's case have proved the stepping stones of thousands to places of dignity and honor, and given them an impetus upward that has rendered their names the synonyms of all that is great and good. In his position as teacher he soon felt the need of a better class of text-books than were then within his reach, for the instruction of pupils in the elementary and fundamental principles of the English Language, and he assumed the task of supplying the deficiency. The result was, "The Gram-

matical Institute of the English Language," published
in three parts. The entire work, however, by means
of a course of evolution, was in a few years reduced
to the well-known "Elementary Spelling Book" of
the present time—a work which was so popular that
up to 1847, 24,000,000 copies of it were published, in
the different forms it assumed under the revision of
its author, with constantly increasing popularity; and,
for a number of years subsequently, the demand
averaged a million copies annually.   In 1862, 41,000-
000 copies had been sold.   Indeed, the entire support
of the lexicographer's family was derived from the
sale of this work, during the twenty years he was engaged in preparing his great American Dictionary,
which was published in 1828.   We all know how uni_
versal was its use until within the past fifteen years,
when it has to some extent been superceded by later,
but I am by no means sure, more worthy, aspirants
for public favor.

Like the intrepid hero whose birthland was the
unpretentious island of Corsica, or Alexander, King
of the insignificant province of Macedon, the English
language, simple in its origin, has nevertheless been a
language of conquest.   Tracing its lineage back to the
Teutonic and Celtic, it claims as its immediate ances-

tors the Angles and Saxon; and, while possessing the
important characteristics of both parents, its more
marked resemblance to the Angles has determined its
name—the Anglican or English language. Besides
this, it receives tribute from perhaps twenty other
tongues, including the French, the Latin and the
Greek—all having more or less influence upon its vo-
cabulary. In fact, it is claimed that its peculiarity
is not so much that it has borrowed words, as that it
has borrowed so many of them. As already stated,
its formative period extended over many centuries; its
slow development being incident to the introduction
of so many elements into its composition in consequence of the frequent changes in the line of its
kings; but its relationship to other tongues and dialects
is too intricate to be given in this place; though what
has been said is relevant in that it serves to show the
difficulties in the way of the great philologist in har-
monizing the discordant elements in termination,
rhythm and euphony, and at the same time giving it
a distinctly American stamp. Indeed, the difficulties
in etymology proved so great that, after spending two
or three years on his great work, he suspended it, and
devoted ten years to its study, spending some months
in Paris and Cambridge consulting men of learning,

and examining books bearing on the subject. The result of this devotion to study, the completion of the great American Dictionary, is the grandest literary achievement of the century. It is the student's treasury; the storehouse from which philosopher, poet and historian draw.

Mr. Webster was an encyclopedia of learning; but his literary record is not circumscribed by his dictionary and spelling book, although, for their influence upon the American and English-speaking world, they are the most important. To these we are indebted for the "remarkable uniformity of pronunciation in our country, which is often spoken of with surprise by English travelers." The success of the Dictionary has verified the author's faith that he had prepared a work that the world will not " willingly let die;" for it has become not only our own standard, but the standard of England, as was shown by the reply of a London bookseller to a gentleman who had called for the best English dictionary: "That," he said, handing him Webster's Unabridged, "is the only real dictionary of the English language, though it was prepared by an American." It was a fine tribute paid by her Majesty's subject to a son of the Republic.

The discipline of Mr. Webster's early years adapted him to his peculiar field of labor. Of a sanguine temperament, his distinguishing traits were enterprise, self-reliance and perseverance. Intimate in his relationship with the leading spirits of the time, such as Alexander Hamilton, John Jay, Oliver Wolcott, Timothy Pickering, and other great men who were active in organizing the new Government, it was in the nature of things that he should undertake to organize a language in harmony with the new mode of thought of our liberty-loving ancestors, and give authority to the Americanisms springing up at the overthrow of tyranny. In truth, in all his works he was conscientiously American, his patriotism asserting itself in every part of his work. In his preface to the American Spelling Book he says: "To diffuse a uniformity and purity of language in America, to destroy the provincial prejudices that originate in the trifling differences of dialects and produce ridicule, to promote the interest of literature and the harmony of the United States, is the most earnest wish of the author; and it is his highest ambition to deserve the approbation and encouragement of his countrymen." Even then he was looking forward to that orthographic reform which our language is gradually undergoing, and dared sometimes brook popular prejudice by introducing words spelled according to the phonetic system, which, at the present time, is gaining favor among "the best speakers and writers," who, according to Noble Butler, are to be accepted as authority; and, when rallied on this innovation, he defended himself by showing that going far enough back we would come on the so-called new form of words in the old English literature; and that he was not inventing, but simply restoring the original orthography of the language. But while yielding deference to old forms in this respect, he never fails in loyalty to his country. Horace E. Scudder says: "The ease with which Webster walked about the Jericho of English lexicography, blowing his trumpet of destruction, was an American ease, born of a sense that America was a continent and not a province. He transferred the capitol of literature from London to Boston or New York or Hartford—he was indifferent so long as it was in America. He thought Washington as good an authority on spelling as Dr. Johnson, and much better than King George. He took the Bible as a book to be used, not as a piece of antiquity to be sheltered in a museum, and with an American practicality set about making it more ser-

viceable in his own way. He foresaw the vast crowds
of American children; he knew that the integrity of
the country was conditioned on the intelligibility of
their votes, and he turned his back to England, less
with indifference to her than absorption in his own
country. He made a speller which has sown votes
and muskets. He made alone a dictionary which ·
has grown, under the impulse he gave it, into a
national encyclopedia, possessing an irresistible mo-
mentum. Indeed, is not the very existence of the
book in its current form a witness to the Americanism
which Webster displayed, only now in a firmer, finer
and more complete form?"

With the completion of his Dictionary, in 1828,
the author considered his literary work done; devoting
his time thereafter mainly to the revision of his early
works. The last labor he performed was the revision
of the Appendix to his greatest work, and the addition
of a few hundred words. This was finished about the
middle of May, 1843—fifteen years from the date of
its first appearance. A few days later, on the 28th of
the same month, full of years and honors, and rejoicing in the hope of a blessed resurrection, he passed
away in the eighty-fifth year of his age.

As a philologist, Noah Webster stands pre-emi-

nently alone; and though others, keeping pace with
the march of human intelligence in all directions,
may further develop and euphonize, may render more
rythmic and beautiful, the English language, no man
will dare contest the honor due him for the funda-
mental work upon which we are rearing the imperishable fabric of American Literature.

LIFE.

Life comes unsought.   It is a precious gift
　From One who wills that all should happy be;
　It is a leaf from an undying tree
Which into nothingness can never drift.
　'Tis of infinity—it is the breath
　Of the Almighty (so the Scripture saith.)
And well worth living, should our souls agree
With the fair terms proposed for you and me;
Death is its shadow, and a mystery
　That hangs about our spirits like a cloud,
　And fills us with vague fears of grave and shroud,
From which we inly shrink.   When it shall lift
　This glorious theme shall all our thoughts engage—
　That we are heirs to such a heritage.

WOMAN'S DEFENSE.

Every star, near and far, without friction or jar,
  Has its sphere, and has never disgraced it;
But if one once should fail, order could not prevail,
  Should it flee from where God's hand had placed it.

     *   *   *

When fealty failed disorder prevailed
  And woman was first to begin it;
With consummate love did Adam resolve
  To follow his wife at the risk of his life,
Of the world, and all that was in it.
The mouth of the Lord hath spoken the word,
  Neither woman nor man can disprove it;
Let it stand; let it be; "He shall rule over thee,"
  Is God's law, and none dare to remove it.

     *   *   *

But woe worth the day, enlarging her sway,
  A woman transcends her dominion;
For honor or pelf unsexing herself,
  And sets 'gainst God's law her opinion
                  —[A. J. HOLT.

The poet, philosopher and the divine,
From "time immemorial," have tried to define,
With logic they deem both conclusive and clear,
What, in the day's parlance, is called woman's sphere

On th' north, south, east, west, it is bounded by Man,
Say they! and the pages of Scripture they scan,
And in tones most exultant claim God gave him pow'r
To "rule over" woman in earth's morning hour.

"It is written" I grant, but defy them to show
Where God said 'twas RIGHT (I am anxious to know)
In the sense it is used! Oft the Scripture we wrest
To prove what we wish—let us give this the test.

The Testaments truly abound, Old and New,
With what man HAS done and what he SHOULD do;
But never once mention that God excused sin,
Tho' they do tell how wayward his children have been.

The Lord simply deigned His own prophet to be
When He thus said to Eve, "He shall rule over thee!"
For only He knew from beginning to end,
How great was the depth to which man would descend!

"He shall rule over thee!" It were easy to prove
The sceptre God meant to be wielded is LOVE;
And all paradoxes we must, if we can,
Thus dovetail if we would decipher His plan.

"He shall rule over thee!" Earth and Heaven rejoice
When in protest a MAN dares to lift up his voice;
While he clings to the doctrine (now laid on the shelf)
That the wife of his bosom's a part of himself.

"He shall rule over thee!"   O, fair daughter of Eve!
Let the tongue of no sophist thy proud heart deceive;
To rule, as men use the term, were an offense
'Gainst Him who ne'er meant it in any such sense.

True, "offenses must come," Jesus said, but we know
Those by whom they do come reap a harvest of woe;
And such is the harvest that's now coming in,
Or I'm too obtuse to explain all this din

About woman's rights and her wrongs and her sphere,
And all the rest of it we constantly hear,
Until it's threadbare—till the cons and the pros
Have verily nothing more new to propose.

"Shall rule!"   What a coward he truly must be
To quote this to one he deems weaker than he!
In physical force this is true, but I ween
In the century current in THOUGHT she's his queen.

Escaped, like a bird, lo! she spreads her light wings,
And startles the world so divinely she sings,
As she moves to the place by her Maker designed,
And stands by man's side in the empire of Mind.

In Literature, Mathematics and Art,
And Science abstruse she has taken such part
That even her "lord" is beginning to feel
That in her he's a rival well worthy his "steel."

And yet, when, her noblest achievement in hand,
The world's verdict waiting she list'ning doth stand,
His qualified praise cuts her soul like a fetter,—
As it seems to imply HE could do so much better!

But let us shift sides, and then "argue the case
Like a lawyer:" Suppose she's abandoned her place,
What tempted her from it? and who is to blame
If she HAS snatched the key to the temple of Fame?

Does he shrink from the issue? Then why did he vex
Her spirit by drawing a line at her sex,
And denying her that which he claimed as his right?
Ah! he did it alone by the virtue (?) of MIGHT!

And if she has wandered away from her sphere,
(A subject involving much doubt) it is clear
When the force is removed that impelled her, why then
She will spring to her own native orbit again.

When man in its true sense shall keep the command:
"Love your wife," and the champion of woman shall
   stand,   `
This unholy war 'twixt the sexes will cease,—
A truce be declared by the Angel of Peace.

Aye, when he shall take the great beam from his eyes,
The cause he will find, with the gravest surprise,
That opened the way for discussions so grim,
Had alike its Omega and Alpha in him!

Howbeit, he never has questioned HIS place?
But, left to MY pencil, a line I will trace,
And by a, perhaps, "new departure," will show
'Twas Adam, NOT Eve, brought about human woe!

Had Adam been standing that day at his post—
That sorrowful day in which Eden was lost;
Eve might have been saved from temptation and fall,
And sin never darkened our planet at all!

MRS. WELTHEA BRYANT LEACHMAN.

"Strange that we should slight the violet till the lovely flower is gone ;
Strange we never prize the music till the sweet-voiced bird is flown ;
And that words which freight our memory with their beautiful perfume
Come to us with sweeter accents through the portals of the tomb."

These words come to me with unusual force this
morning in connection with the name of Mrs. Welthea
Bryant Leachman, of Dallas, whose recent death has
cast a gloom over many a heart that her songs were
wont to soothe. On Christmas Eve of 1884, I came
to Dallas, a stranger. A year later, under date of
January 1, 1886, I first read a poem from the pen of
this gifted woman, entitled "The Passing of the
Year." I at once said to a friend that "Dallas has at
least one true poet;" but I could scarcely credit the
fact that I had lived so near her all these months and
not heard of her. It seemed strange that one so
gifted should be so little known. I made frequent
inquiries about her, but could learn little more than
that she was a resident of the city, and sometimes
contributed to the local press. From a stray copy of
the "Farm and Ranch" I learned that she edited
the Household Department of that journal; and also

her place of residence. From that time I decided I
would call upon her, and, if possible, secure her as a
regular contributor to the "Lone Star Magazine;" but
I postponed the visit from time to time until, alas,
it was too late. Now and then through the past year
the melody of her songs has reached my ear; but on
February 3d the song was suddenly hushed, the sweet
lyre unstrung, and the gifted poet passed into the
Land through whose gates no one whose ear is not attuned to Song shall ever enter.

Yesterday I visited the stricken home to gather
such items of interest as always attach to the home-
life of the true poet. A shadow hangs over the pretty
cottage, nestled away in a quiet street, and lingers in
the heart of the bereaved household—a shadow that
will never be lifted in this life, though under the
soothing influence of the great healer, Time, the tenderness of the wound will somewhat abate. But hidden away in the heart is a void that cannot be filled
—a memory sweeter and dearer and tenderer than
anything life can offer; while a hope, born of sorrow,
stretches away as a rainbow of promise into the
beautiful Beyond. Here and there were pointed out
evidences of the poet's handiwork. I especially
noticed a piece of unfinished crochet work; and an

herbarium, with some of the collections not yet fastened to the leaves. It is almost filled, and contains a great variety of specimens, many of them gathered from distant places; among them several kinds of field ferns, from Block Island and about Boston. The furniture is in perfect harmony with the size of the rooms and general appearance of the cottage, and everywhere are evidences of the refined taste of the poet. In conversation with Mr. Leachman, who seems truly inconsolable, he said he felt completely broken up; that time did not lessen his consciousness of loss, adding, " If she had been only an ordinary woman, with ordinary tastes, I think I could have borne it better." I can enter into this feeling. I, too, once had a dear and gifted friend called away in the beauty of youth and intellectual vigor, when the promise of fame—the far-off goal of ambition—was looming up in the distance. She, like our author, was born in Texas; but in the South many of the sons and daughters of Song die young. For evidence read the " Poets and Poetry of Texas." Paul H. Hayne is among the exceptions. Contrast these with the Northern poets. Literary life in congenial atmosphere—I mean among appreciative readers—is conducive to longevity. Ah, truly God's handiwork is

not to be despised. He makes the Poet and places
him in this land of almost tropical beauty, of which
he sings so delightfully; for the true child of Song can
no more still the music in his breast than the brook
can cease to flow or the flowers to bloom. The song
sings itself, but it will not do such prosy work as feed
and clothe the singer; and our people have set their
affections too much on the alluring charms of Mam-
mon to leave any room for thought of the song bird
that is helplessly beating its wings against the cage
and sighing for freedom. Truly, it does seem that
Adversity has set a mark upon our most gifted writers
and when the pent-up song does burst forth it comes
to us full of pathos; but alas, it too often falls on unheeding ears. No wonder the sensitive spirit droops
under such surroundings, and that the great Father
reaches down and takes it to himself. But He sends
another and still another, and, after awhile, I think
the South will throw off her yoke of bondage to Gold
and stretch forth her hand to sustain these God-sent
messengers.

Welthea Bryant, a distant relative of William
Cullen Bryant, was born at Galveston, Texas, December 25, 1847. A short time afterward her parents
moved to Corpus Christi, near which place her father,

Major Charles G. Bryant, was killed by the Indians in 1848—only a year later. Her early life was passed here amid somewhat exciting scenes. As poets are born such, it is but natural that the poetic faculty should develop early. This was true in her case, though it seems she wrote nothing worthy of preservation until she was about fifteen years of age. In 1860 she was sent to New Orleans to school. During the blockade she escaped from the city and was placed under the care of an aunt in Boston, to whom she became much attached. Their affection and correspondence continued through her life. Miss Bryant was married twice—first to a Mr. Graham, in 1863. She was married next in 1875, to Mr. J. S. Leachman, of Dallas, a gentleman of taste and refinement. She leaves but one child, a fragile little boy of five summers, several little ones having preceded her to the Spirit world.

It is with reverent fingers I turn the leaves of her scrap-book to glean the rich gems that sparkle here and there in so unworthy a setting—gems worthy to be bound in clasps of gold. It is not classical learning, nor Shakesperean style, nor æsthetic culture that makes the true poet; but that intangible something that in its tender pathos appeals to every heart,

and awakes a feeling of common brotherhood. This
vein characterized Mrs. Leachman's earliest published
poems and·at once attracted the favorable notice of
the critics of that great center of culture—Boston.
"Not Dead, but Gone Before," is worthy the author of
"Thanatopsis," and was written when our poet was
quite young—little older than was Mr. Bryant when
he wrote the lines which have wedded his name to
immortality. I reproduce the poem in full:

"NOT DEAD—BUT GONE BEFORE."

They press around me in a glorious band—
  Shadowed upon the camera of thought ;
                They bend
Unseen; their embassies of hand to hand
  And soul to soul, throng in unsought;
                And friend
And foe meet and embrace and glide away,
Performing deeds of love, nor falter by the way.

A sweeping host—I see them hurrying by—
  No star-crowned, white winged IDLE angels they,
                But souls—
Souls that must tireless search the earth and sky,
  Eternity and time and dreamless day,
                And poles
Of other, brighter, holier worlds than these,
Beyond our summer skies or summer seas.

Around above me, and the air is full
  Of guests, plucked from the highways of the land,
           And they,
Fresh from the glories of Bethsaida's pool,
  'Mid resurrection of soul, heart and hand,
           For aye
Feast from the tables of the wondrous Lamb,
With brow serene and spirits pure and calm

The friendless and forsaken—orphans lone
  And frail hearts that have bent beneath their woe
           And misery;
Stray waifs in life;—mother and sire and son,
  Virtue and crime and innocence—and lo!
           Eternity
Whispers around me that the solemn air
Is partly mine, for those I love are there!

Not dead—but gone before! A little while
  When standing on the brink of endless day
           And love,
Unfelt, their gentle touch, unseen, the'r smile
  Shall trace beyond the shoals of doubt, the way
           Above;—
Mayhap some little babe with guileless hand
Will catch our wakening in the Summer land!

Not dead—but gone before! Ah! dreamless sleep!
  Ah! resurrection from the silent tomb
           To Life Eternal,
Unveil thy mystery, that those who weep
  Shall quick embrace thee, so their souls may bloom
          In bliss supernal!
Not dead—but gone before! A peerless band—
The Wisdom-seekers of the better land!

Ah! guardian one who dwelleth with the pure,
  Hymning thy glories o'er each new born soul,
          I plead;
Teach me thy simple way,—unveil the lure
  Which waves of doubt and fear around me roll;
          I need
Thy grasp upon the helm, thy wondrous lore
To prove THOU ART NOT DEAD—BUT GONE BEFORE.

Had the author of these beautiful lines remained in that great literary centre, under the shadow of Harvard, with the intellectual atmosphere pervading it, and with the healthful encouragement that gives zest to earnest effort, strength to imagination, and assists in developing the loftier sentiments of the soul, it is probable she would have taken her place before the world as one of the finest writers of the present time. Indeed, I think if her poems could be published as the literary remains recently brought to light of some one of our most distinguished authors, they would not only create a favorable sensation among the critics, but would doubtless be classed among such writer's best production; not that the critics are at fault, but that the tyrant Circumstance, has prevented these exquisite gems being brought to their notice; for Circumstance wields a sceptre before which the millions bow, while the hearts of its un-

happy victims pine in secret over the dream of what
" might have been."

There is a pathos in our Poet's song which tells
that the deep silences of her breast have been touched
by sorrow; but the discipline of sorrow is sometimes
necessary to the development of true genius. It is
the cry of the bruised spirit as it " passes under the
rod," that awakes a sympathetic chord in the great
heart of humanity ;

> Immortal and pure, methinks that Song
>   Is an Angel that walks the world of men;
> And every emotion, deep and strong,
>   Breathes of her presence, herself unseen;
> But the Poet chosen and set apart
>   To give true voice to this sacred guest,
> Must feel, if he'd stir the great world's heart,
>   The sting of the thorn in his own breast.

I have only space to give a stanza here and there
from her exquisite poems, in doing which I am fully
conscious that I cannot do the author justice, as one
must see a work of Art in its entirety to truly appreciate it. Listen to the plaint of the mother-heart
over the loss of one of her nestlings :

> "The winds sigh on thro' the languid hours,
>   And the moonbeams silver the lea,

And the eyes we loved have oped on a land
  Far over Eternity's Sea;
The frail hand, grasping the bending oar,
  Has stiffened in Death's embrace,
And a bark swept on to an unknown shore
  Where we worship our Father's face;
And we'll list no more for the bird like voice
Or the footstep that made our heart rejoice."

From "The Hour Glass," a tender little poem of seven stanzas, I select two:

" Drop by drop have the little sands
  Run down the glass in my idle hands;
One by one have the moments flown.
Till the hour has come and the hour has gone;
1 shift the motion, and down they go,
Dropping so noiseless and sure and slow.

" Some day my heart, in its frame of clay,
  Shall cease to beat, and the light of day
Will come no more to my weary eyes,
Nor my tired lips give forth smiles or sighs,
And the red drops pulsing within my veins
Will still 'neath the quiver of dying pains."

This last stanza, so full of premonition and pathos, comes like a dirge to the ear to-day. It is dated August, 1886, less than a year ago.

Among the many literary remains before me, there are several poems possessing perhaps more power, reaching greater depths and loftier heights, than those from which I have quoted, though not perhaps more beautiful ; but fragmentary quotations would prove inadequate to express their beauty, and so I desist, trusting that some kind hand will gather them at an early day and present them to the world in a handsome volume. Among these is that exquisite poetical Address to the Texas Veterans, which has elicited so many enconiums from the Press. Mrs. Welthea F. Snow, of Boston, an aunt of our Poet, writing to Mrs. Leachman's brother, Mr. W. N. Bryant, of Dallas, says :

"It is a bitter disappointment to me—her untimely death. Her talents were beginning to be recognized both North and South as brilliant gifts, and I felt both pleased and proud of her—hoped she would make her mark in the literary world, and honor the name of Bryant, our illustrious predecessor. A gentleman friend of mine, an accepted poet, to whom I showed her poetic 'Address to the Veterans of Texas,' said : 'Why! this is worthy of the name of Bryant! It will compete with his word-pictures in finish and beauty.' But she had limited means and opportunities in this life. Where she is, there is rest for the weary and glorious liberty—she can grow and shine."

Yes, she can grow, for she is "Not dead—but gone before" to the Land of Life and Light and Song; and if our tears fall over her untimely grave, let them fall for "ourselves" who are left to loiter on amid the shadows, and—not for her.

Another appreciative friend writes: "She had genius, and with happy influences and better sur-roundings, she would have taken high rank among literary people; as it was, she had done wonders. May the earth lie lightly on her grave."

So far, I have considered Mrs. Leachman alone as a poet; but while her genius shines more re-splendently in this field, her prose sketches sparkle with happy thought and beautiful imagery. Illustra-tive of this I copy a part of a letter written from Galveston to the Household department of the Farm and Ranch. Standing on the seashore watching the ships sailing away from the fair City by the Sea, she writes:

"I have watched them sailing on and on, out of sight, fading away on the dim distant horizon; the star of hope that shone so bravely above them, sud-denly went down, and all was darkness and confusion and despair. Sailing, sailing away, they bore all that was best of life, and love and hope, and youth's

flowery gems, and they have never come back to me.
And days and nights for many years I looked and I
searched the shore in vain for my ships, but alas!
none ever came. As I thought of the treasures they
held, dreamy smiles would chase over my lips, and I
would whisper of all that would be mine 'when my
ships came in.' But, ah, me! they have never come.
Somewhere else, either they are still sailing, sailing
away, seeking gold and jewels rare, or, with battered
hulk and tattered sails, they are plunging through
foaming breakers, and slowly yielding the last rem-
nant of hope, while above the broken mast a beautiful dove is sighing as if saying :

'Leave me alone! the dream is my own, and my heart is full of rest.'

And so it is—full of rest! They are gone, but some
day the fragments will come back.   I see plainly the
star of hope still shining, and my heart is full of
rest."

Yes, her "heart is full of rest" now. She has
sailed away to find the lost ships, full-freighted,
safely anchored, and

"No storms ever beat on that beautiful shore in the far-away Home of
the Blest."

But the songs she has sung will remain with us.
They may never be found in gilded volume in the

world-renowned library ; though in memory of the
fact that she was a daughter of Texas, and as a
tribute to the merit of her beautiful Address to the
Veterans, the people of the State should see that
these gems are enshrined in a worthy setting. But
should this not be done, treasured by loving hands,
they will live in scrapbooks to soothe weary hearts on
through the years—precious melodies sweeping out
to "Eternity's Sea."

THE LAND OF REST.

There is a country just beyond earth's shadows,
　Where beauteous trees and flowers perennial grow;
And thro' its sunlit vales and grassy meadows,
　Meandering streams of living waters flow;
There pain and grief no more disturb the breast—
It is the saint's bright home, the Land of Rest.

Then Christian-traveler thro' this world of sorrow,
　Let smiles break o'er thy face instead of tears;
The night will ne'er close on the glad To-Morrow,
　Whose dawn shall usher in eternal years;
The sun of life but fades along the west
To rise in beauty on the Land of Rest.

Tho' dark the way, and the path long in turning,
   And tho' thy feet are tired and sandal-worn;
And tho' thy weary heart for Home is yearning,
   And tho' thy breast by many a pang is torn;
The Lord is leading thee, and knoweth best
By WHAT WAY thou shouldst reach the Land of Rest.

"For good" remember, "all things work together"
   To the dear children of the Father's love;
And accidents can ne'er befall them, whether
   'Long open paths or thro' dark ways they move;
They are His care; when seeming most opprest
Their feet still tend toward the Land of Rest.

The mother even may forget her darling,
   But O, OUR FATHER ne'er forgets his own;
Tho' lost amid dense woods or pathless jungles,
   Or wandering on the mountain tops alone;
He fain would clasp them to His loving breast,
And HE WILL bring them to the Land of Rest.

Some may plan badly; oft "wood, hay or stubble"
   The place of grander edifice supplies;
And the poor builder's heart is bowed with trouble
   That his life-structure points not to the skies;

"These works will all be burned"—nor stand the test;
"Saved as by fire" he'll reach the Land of Rest.

But he whose will is lost in God's; who never
   Turns to the right or left along the way;
Whose "heart is fixed" and grateful to the Giver
   Of great or smaller blessings—come which may:
Will have, as the reward of faith and zest,
ABUNDANT entrance to the Land of Rest.

Then christian-traveler thro' this world of sorrow,
   Let smiles break o'er thy face instead of tears;
The night will ne'er close o'er the bright To-Morrow,
   Whose dawn shall usher in eternal years;
Life's cloud-dimmed sun but fades along the west
To rise in GLORY on the Land of Rest.

————

SAVED.

Shipwrecked and cast upon a barren Land,
   Alone, I watch the earth and sea and sky;
   The storm still rages and the waves beat high,
   But far or near there's nothing greets the eye
That breathes of safety; even the bit of strand
Beneath my feet is simply treach'rous sand.

With lifted hands I wildly beat the air,
And send to Heaven an agonizing prayer;
When lo! beyond the tempest and the mist,
A stretch of open sky, like amethyst,
And in the midst a beautiful bright star,
Thro' the pure ether gleaming from afar,
Shows at my feet a ship, with sails all set,
Steered by the Pilot of Gennesaret.

WELCOME TO KENTUCKIANS.

[This poem appeared in the *Dallas News* on the 23d of October, 1890, as a greeting to the writer's compatriots on "Kentucky Day" at the fair.]

Kentuckians! We welcome you
From the dear home afar;—
Throned in Our Country's galaxy
There shines no brighter star;
Tho' severed long, its light still cheers,
Undimmed by distance or the years.

But while 'twixt us remains a tie
The years can ne'er despoil,
Kentucky has a colony
Growing on Texas soil;—

Exiles by choice, with gladness they
Would greet you on this glorious day.

Kentucky! How our heartstrings thrill
     At mention of the name!
Far as the English tongue is heard,
     Extends her sons' just fame
For chivalry, in peace or war,
And daughters lovely past compare.

When erst along our hills and vales
     Sounded war's rude alarms,
Her sons were ready at the word
     To buckle on their arms;—
To the fair South one band went forth,
One joined the armies of the North.

And it seemed meet that on her soil
     The serried hosts divide,
And a great army, brave and true,
     Enlist on either side,
Since from her breast the Chiefs were sprung
Whose fame is spread by every tongue.

There Lincoln, who the Northland's name
     And honor held in trust;

And the great Davis, by their birth,
    E'er consecrate her dust;
And well may we Kentuckians boast
Of each—each in himself a host.

While yet we mourn the recent loss
    Of the great Southland Chief,
Time for the martyred President
    Has modified our grief;
Albeit above their honored graves
The same bright banner lightly waves.

But other figures proudly stand
    Before our eyes to-day—
Blackburn, Carlisle, Knott, Watterson—
    Compatriots of Clay;
Whose words and deeds the hopes beget
Kentucky's star shall never set.

But ere this orb the zenith reached
    Another had its birth—
The bright Lone Star, whose rosy light
    Encompasseth the earth;
And whose brave sons, a gallant band,
Have won renown in every land.

In her, behold our second love—
    Texas! by every mouth
Proclaimed, as golden crowned she stands,
    The Empire of the South;
And yet, as said by one of old,
Of her "the half has ne'er been told."

Now, once again, we welcome you
    From the old home afar;
Our Country's brilliant firmament
    Claims not a brighter star:—
Shrined in our hearts it fills a place
Not even Texas can efface.

A RAINY DAY.

How very dreary the earth is looking just now!
How fitfully the clouds sweep across the heavens, now
bursting forth in torrents, now distilling a gentle
mist, but none the less obscuring the beauties of the
sky, and hopelessly veiling their proverbial silver
lining. And yet, I can recall a time when a day of
rain and storm came like a ray of sunlight into my
life, breaking its monotony, and furnishing a respite

from the sometimes wearisome task of teaching " the
young idea how to shoot"—a day of rain, when, em-
broidery in hand, I could sit at my window, and
watch the changing clouds, and dream—such dreams
as only come once in a life; youthful dreams, with
no shadows flitting over them to obscure their beauty;
beautiful dreams, in which I had little time to in-
dulge in my chosen avocation. Still, there are many
pleasures connected with this noble calling. While it
is true that one often meets with those who not only
expect their teacher to instruct them, but to learn (?)
them—those who have never entered even the vesti-
bule of STUDY, nor penetrated its twilight, much less
stood in its noontide glare and beheld the bounteous
intellectual feast there spread;(a sight which awakens
in the aspiring mind a perception of such vast possibilities, such visions of the attainable, and gives it
such an overwhelming consciousness of its impotence,
in the short span of this life, to grasp all it were even
possible to reach) one finds others walking cheerfully
along the paths of Knowledge, drinking of every
stream, plucking its richest fruits, inhaling the fragrance of its sweetest flowers—their minds developing and expanding as the vast expanse of its landscape opens up before them; and, nerved with the re-

solve which makes heroes, they place their mark high on the scroll of Fame, and set forward with determination to reach it. Do we wonder that they succeed ? Why should we ? It is those who have no object in view that faint and drop by the wayside. It is those who have no goal to win that are overcome by the noontide heat.

In those far-away days—so far away it would almost seem like a century to a young girl of eighteen, if counted forward; for more than a score of years have numbered their fleeting moments on the dial of life since then—I particularly recall the face of one little girl, Sarah Hainelyn, whose love of books was a source of wonder to those who knew her surroundings. Scarcely ten summers had passed over her golden head; or rather, I should say winters, for her mother was a confirmed invalid, and her father a no less confirmed drunkard; and, although there were older children in the family, the burden of the household rested upon her young shoulders. Notwithstanding all this, and the straightened circumstances of her life, she was usually first in the class room. Always with lessons well prepared, she braved the inclemencies of the seasons, wading through frost and snow, with bare feet, and no warp to shield her slight form from the bitter cold of that rigorous climate, she never wearied in the pursuit of knoweledge. As gold is not all confined to the mines, but is sometimes found in unexpected or out-of-the-way places, so rare jewels like this are sometimes found in the humblest stations of life. She seemed called and chosen and faithful to the work before her, and I trust that in some one's crown of rejoicing, in the great Hereafter, "she may shine as a star forever and ever."

A rainy day! How it stirs old memories, and how my thoughts have wandered! But Thought at best is capricious and untamable. And then, who is not glad to get away, if only in dreams, from such a day as this? The clouds have hung over us until even a glimpse of the sun would send a thrill of joy throughout the house. We scarcely noticed it when the whole earth was bathed in its golden beams, but now we truly realize that "blessings brighten as they take their flight," and are ready to echo the sentiment of Tennyson, that—

"A sorrow's crown of sorrow is remembering happier things."

Looking through the clouds that have enveloped us, mentally and physically, for many days, we are apt to conclude that earth has more of clouds than clear sky, more of shadow than sunlight. And yet, this is a mistake. There are more bright, beautiful days than days of rain, morally as well as physically, and we must take life as it comes. We must walk with Lazarus and the publican through the valley of Humility and Sorrow, if from the summit of Mount Nebo we would catch a glimpse of the Promised Land.

WORDS OF JESUS.

" 'Tis expedient for you that I go away; "
    How these words, with their tender tone,
  Must have thrill'd the souls of the faithful few
    So soon to be left alone.

" It is best for you, for the world, that I
    Return to My Father's Home;
  I tell you th' truth—if I go not away
    The Comforter will not come.

" Because I have said these things to you,
    Sorrow hath filled your heart;
  But the work that I came to do is done;
    'Tis my hour—I must depart;

"Yet, Father, if poss'ble, let this cup pass!"
　　(And the Only Begotten Son
Sweat drops of crimson;) "Nevertheless,
　　Not Mine, but Thy will be done."

The anguish pass'd with these trustful words,
　　And the swift-winged Cherubim
Came down the blue stairway of the skies
　　To minister unto Him.

And th' calmness of Heaven soothed the breasts
　　(Such as the world ne'er knew)
Of his sorrowing friends as he gently said,
　　"But My peace I leave with you."

"Not as the world (oh, no, thank God!)
　　Giveth, give I unto you;
My gifts are beyond regret or recall;
　　'Tis the Father's will I do.

"In the world ye will tribulation have,"
　　(But your hearts with this peace impearl'd,
Will be strong for life's conflict.) "Be of good
　　　　cheer—
　　I have overcome the world!"

COL. JOHN C. McCOY.

We sought to stay
An angel on the earth—a spirit ripe
For Heaven; and Mercy, in her love, refused;
Most merciful oftimes when seeming least;
Most gracious oft when seeming most to frown.
—[POLLOK.

Speaking from a large observation and experience, Horace Mann has truly said that "Biography, especially of the great and good who have risen by their own exertions to eminence and usefulness, is an inspiring and ennobling study, its direct tendency being to reproduce the excellence it records." With this view of the subject, it is not strange that no sooner does a good man pass from the stage of action in this life, than the biographer is ready with his pen to catch the reflex of the glory which crowned his life, and trace it with all its living radiance upon the pages of history, as a guide to others who would aspire to worthy heights in the intellectual or moral universe. Indeed, the arena upon which the drama of most heroic lives is enacted is too narrow to complete the mission it was designed they should fulfill, without the aid of the pen and press to place the "usefulness of their examples " before the public.

From the vast amount of this, the "most universally pleasant and profitable of all reading " constantly being issued, a casual observer might pronounce this peculiarly an age of biography—an age in which not only the dead, but the living also, share in this distinction. Any one coming before the world now, as a representative of literature, art, science, oratory, philanthropy, the drama, or as an illustration of the "faith that works by love," or in any other way contributing to its pleasure, amusement or edification, at once awakens in the breast a desire to know something of his birth, parentage, surroundings and private life. But this is by no means peculiar to our time. Nearly seventeen centuries before the dawn of the Christian era, when David, standing between the armies of Israel and the mighty hosts of the Philistines, and scorning the heavy armor of Saul, single-handed slew the Chieftain who had "defied the armies of the living God," we hear the King of Israel asking Abner, the Captain of his hosts, whose son the stripling is; and, not satisfied with a negative answer, he seeks the youth himself, and asks, "Whose son art thou?" And the reply, "I am the son of

Jesse, the Bethlehemite" demonstrates that then, as now, highest worth was to be found in the lowly walks of life. We do not wonder at the question. The heroism of that act stands unparalleled, and has doubtless served as an inspiration to thousands, where deeds of valor were to be done. Nor is this an idle, but rather, a commendable curiosity. We find this verified in the fact· that the genealogy of the most important personages mentioned in the Divine Record is given, with few exceptions; among these, that of Elijah the Tishbite, and of Melchisedec, around whose origin is spread a veil which eternity alone can lift. And so when those whom we love or admire passes from the visible world into the great Beyond, as a last tribute to their memory and their worth, it is with confident, yet trembling hands, we lift the pall from their sacred Past, and with reverent fingers turn the pages of the volume written to its close amid scenes perhaps familiar to us.

There is one thought impressed upon the mind in reviewing the actions of men who have distinguished themselves, either as recorded in history, or as exhibited in person or in our midst—the thought that they were so especially adapted, as if by force of destiny, to the times in which they lived. That

Circumstance has much to do with deciding a man's field of action must be admitted, but one who has attained the full stature of Christian manhood realizes that there is a Power superior to, and which controls, even Circumstance; and so the fact remains that when a great work is to be done, whether that of discovering a continent, developing the resources of a wilderness, founding a colony, chaining the lightning, inventing the telegraph, or any other work within the compass of human powers, the man is found ready for the time and work. We find this illustrated in Columbus, through whose discovery a place of refuge was prepared for the oppressed of all lands; and in Washington, so worthily and fittingly called the Father of his Country, since he spent his life in paternal guardianship and solicitude for the land to which he had given the devotion of a parent, and, who dying, left no son upon whom the people, as an expression of their deep gratitude to himself and devotion to his memory, might place the insignia of royalty. Franklin and Fulton and Stevenson and Whitney and Morse, and many others whose names and works time fails us to mention, stand before the world as illustrious witnesses of the truth that a Divine Architect is fitting every man to his time and work.

And so in a narrower but perhaps not less important sphere than was respectively occupied by those whose names are mentioned, is the assertion again verified in Col. John C. McCoy, whose death, on April 30, 1877, cast a deep shadow over the city so much indebted to him for its foundation, development and present prosperity. Col. McCoy, born in Clark county, Indiana, September 28, 1819, was of Scotch-Irish descent. His father was a farmer, and from an early age until he was fifteen, the son was a faithful laborer on the farm, during which period we have not been able to gain any information regarding his educational advantages. But at the expiration of this time his father moved to Charleston, and he entered the Clark County Seminary, presided over by one of the finest instructors of the day. He made rapid progress in his studies, and a year later was matriculated at Wilmington Seminary, of which his brother, Isaac McCoy, was President. Three years in school ending his career as a student of text books, he entered on the active duties of life. For a number of years he was variously engaged, accepting employment wherever an opening occurred, whether as deputy county clerk, enrolling officer, bookkeeper, or in any other capacity; always proving himself trust-

worthy and capable; in the meantime, in the inter-
vals of leisure he could command, pursuing the
study of law, which he had chosen as a profession.
In 1841 he obtained his diploma, and was enrolled as
counselor and advocate in Kentucky and Indiana.
He practiced with signal success for about three
years, when his restless spirit, pining for the scenes
of excitement incident to frontier life, he decided to
accept a position offered him as sub-agent and sur-
veyor for Peter's Colony in Texas; and on the 12th of
December, 1844, he turned his face toward the broad
plains which were to be the theater of his greatest
privations, labors and successes.

Trusting to maps and charts, sent out then as·
now, to lure the unsuspecting victim into unoccupied
fields, he came to Dallas to find, instead of the well-
built town so beautifully delineated on the chart, a
single log cabin occupied by a recluse whose name,
John Neely Bryan, will be preserved in history as
that of the first settler in the metropolis of Texas.
He was dressed in buckskin leggings, his feet encased
in moccasins, and a blanket coat made in what was
termed high water style. The young lawyer received
a cordial welcome, but to one possessed of refined
tastes and accustomed to all the social amenities of

cultivated society, as he had been, it must have been a severe disappointment. His great soul, however, was equal to the occasion; and we find him entering with zest upon his new sphere of duties.

As an orator it is said by one who has heard him from the forum that "he was exceedingly graceful in his delivery, never failing to entrance by his cultivated thoughts, flowing sentences and classical allusions, all those whose happy privilege it was to hear him" But the secret of his success as a lawyer lay in the justice of the cause he would advocate; his deep earnestness, and the truthfulness of his heart as expressed in his words, his countenance and his gestures. In person he was "exceedingly neat and even fastidious, and delighted in nothing so much as the simple elegancies of life that add convenience and comfort to the cheerfulness they afford."

He was ever a friend and patron of literature and literary institutions; and from the establishment of the Dallas City Public Library, of which institution he was one of the founders, he was President until his death, ever contributing freely both time and money to its maintenance; and the badge of mourning adopted by its members on his death attest their consciousness of the loss they have sustained. That his intellectual endowments were of a very high order is shown in the taste and judgment displayed in the selection of books, his library being one of the finest private collections in the State, consisting of standard works and the best productions of recent authors. One has said of him that "he may be justly regarded as the best posted scholar in the classical, as he is in the general, literature of the day, anywhere to be met with in this section of our State, which, considered in connection with the fact that he had passed his palmiest days in the service of all those dangers, hardships and demands, incident to frontier life, must reflect additional credit upon his tastes, his natural endowments and his attainments; for there was a time running over many years of his life when he never saw a book or newspaper, yet amid all these wild scenes and dangerous excitements he never lost sight of the Muses, who constantly ministered to his thoughts; and in his own words, he ' has experienced his greatest pleasures when communing with the stars as he lay stretched upon his single blanket on the prairies; and in his travels he has never heard anything so grand as the soft winds of the whispering forest, or seen anything so pure as the distilled dews that tremble upon the grasses of the boundless

plains.'" As so beautifully expressed by James G.
Percival, he realized that

> "The world is filled with poetry—the air
> Is living with its spirit; and the waves
> Dance to the music of its melodies,
> And sparkle in its brightness; earth is veiled
> And mantled with its beauty; and the walls
> That close the universe with crystal in
> Are eloquent with voices that proclaim
> The unseen glories of immensity,
> In harmonies too perfect and too high
> For aught but beings of celestial mould,
> And speak to man in one eternal hymn
> Of fadeless beauty and unyielding power.'

Col. McCoy was married in 1851 to Miss Cora
McDermett whose father had emigrated from Penn-
sylvania to Texas in 1846. The marriage was an ex-
ceptionably happy one, and of their home it has been
said that it "was the home of gayety and mirth and
pleasure, and was frequented by those who loved to
steal away from the cares of busy life, and for an
hour to realize that the world is still beautiful, notwithstanding the trials that sometimes overtake the
toilers in its active scenes." But human joy is ever
evanescent. Scarcely two years passed over this
happy home when the young wife, in the first joy of
motherhood, was laid to rest, and beside her the

sweet unconscious babe that was destined to never know the joys or the sorrows of this life. Through all the years that passed over his head leaving their traces on his silken hair, and on the yielding and venerable form, his heart remained true to its one great, imperishable love, and manifested its devotion to its object in the tender care bestowed on the six orphaned brothers and sisters of his wife, whom he reared and educated at his own expense, and fitted for spheres of usefulness. And it may be that the unbounded love he had for children, and which found expression in so many tender ways, especially in the joyous Christmas-times, and which was extended to all, irrespective of caste or social condition, had its birth in the grave of the little one laid to rest under the daisies so many years ago; while the unobtrusive charity so earnestly commended by the Master when he said "Let not the left hand know what the right hand doeth," which he so freely dispensed in quiet ways and on deserving objects, had its roots in the stream of sorrow sprung so long ago in his own sympathizing heart.

But the springs of joy and sorrow flow side by side in the human breast, and in his social life Col. McCoy was always cheerful; and from the time the religious side of his character was developed, about seven years ago, his life was one of trust. and perfect rest. Such a life as his is rarely lived out in a community—so full of years and dignity and usefulness; with so few blemishes, even before Religion had traced its benign and radiating features upon his genial spirit. He passed away when a field of labor, whose boundaries lay beyond our sight, seemed out-stretched and awaiting his ever willing and ever faithful hands; and at a time when, as his pastor, Rev. R. T. Hanks, so truly said, he was so much needed, we could scarcely believe he could die. And could the prayers and tears of his friends have availed, his place among us would not be vacant now ; but the great Arbiter of human destiny knows best—

> "The Christian cannot die before his time;
> The Lord's appointment is the servant's hour."

The character for generosity and kindliness of heart which he eminently sustained, is beautifully illustrated in the incident or two here given : On their way from Indiana to their point of destination in this State, after leaving Galveston and traveling some distance by a rude conveyance, one of the party to which Col. McCoy belonged was taken dangerously ill and had to be left at a house by the wayside. Before parting from him Col. McCoy gave him the last money he had—fifty cents; adding such words of encouragement as he could under the circumstances. There was a young lady at this house; and he told the sick man that he would get well, marry her and become a rich planter. The young man was exceedingly offended at such jesting at a time when he believed himself at the very point of death, and expressed himself so in language much more emphatic than elegant. The evident intention of Col. McCoy was to arouse the invalid from a state of despondency, in which generous design he was doubtless successful; and the sequel demonstrates the correctness of his thoughtless prophecy—the gentleman got well, married the young lady, became a wealthy planter, and, years after, was honored by being elected as a representative to the Legislature. The second incident is this :

Soon after his death, a woman from the country called at the office of Capt. McCoy, the nephew and partner of the late Col. McCoy. She said that some time ago she had a case in court, but, not having the ability to employ an attorney, when her case was called she appeared without any one to advocate her claims, when Col. McCoy volunteered his services and gained the case, the verdict being rendered in her favor. She seemed deeply grieved at her benefactor's death, and said that she would ever hold him in grateful rememberance. As an evidence of the sincerity and unobtrusiveness of such kindly deeds his best friends knew nothing of this last circumstance till since his death, when the recipient of his kindness related it. But his deeds of love are now done—"he rests from his labors and his works do follow him."

At the time of his death Col. McCoy was chairman of two deliberative bodies or committees appointed by the Church to look after the interests of the new house of worship of the First Baptist Church of Dallas, then in the process of erection; and was also teacher of an interesting class of girls in the Sabbath School. The floral offering made by these girls to decorate his grave was a tender tribute to his memory; while the honorable position he had attained in the benevolent orders of the State—the Masonic, Knight Templar and others; the number of members of these respective fraternities from a distance who were present to take part in the obsequies, together with the large assemblage of the citizens in attendance on the imposing ceremonies at the church, attest the high esteem in which he was held by all classes.

The scene is closed upon a noble life, the curtain lifted between the Seen and Unseen, and the venerable form has passed into the mystery of the Unknown Country toward which we are all moving. But he went not

> " Like the quarry slave at night,
> Scourged to his dungeon; but sustained and soothed
> By an unfaltering trust, approached his grave
> Like one who wraps the drapery of his couch
> Around him and lies down to pleasant dreams."

THE GIFT RECLAIMED.

[These lines are designed to keep in rememberance some of the sweet sayings of little Johnny C. Taggart, grand-nephew and namesake of Col. John C. McCoy.]

From the Court of Love, one gladsome day,
A beautiful Angel bent his way
Toward the earth; and to his breast
A baby-cherub was lightly prest.

Anon he entered a lovely home
Where the door ajar seemed beck'ning, Come!
And laid the little one, pure and fair,
In the arms of a mother waiting there.

For three short years on a human breast
This child of the skies was soothed to rest;
But weary and sick one July day
On a bed of pain the little one lay.

The mother, her bosom all athrill,
And her very heart beats almost still,
Bent near and prayed the little one tell
"What he'd do if God didn't make him well."

And now his beautiful, cheerful faith,
Exalts him above the fear of death;
And into his eyes the glad light springs
As he answers, "Jesus will give me wings!

"And Mamma, in that bright world of joy,
Will Uncle Mac know your little boy?
I shall know him by his snow-white vest,
And the whiskers flowing over his breast!"

Ah! little thought they who bent to hear
The little "white wings" were quite so near;
But that eventide he took his flight
To his native realm of love and light.

As near he drew to the pearly gate,
Where, with folded wings, the sentries wait,
A smile of ineffable brightness spread
His pale face o'er, and the sweet lips said :

"Look, mamma! papa!"   The clear blue eyes
Had caught a glimpse of the Paradise
Which stretches away beyond the Blue—
The home of the pure and good and true.

While one little hand the bosom prest
Where the baby-head was wont to rest,
The other swept back the viewless screen
Which veils the beauties "eye hath not seen."

When into his heart the sad thought crept
Of the pain of leaving those who wept,
His child-faith triumphed in the refrain :
"You'll all come, too!"—yes, they'll meet again.

And then an Angel, veiled in the mist,
Swept down, by the heavenly breezes kiss'd,
Caught the darling up past the realm of air,
And left but the cold-clay garments there.

In the stricken home is an empty chair,
But a seat is filled in a Home more fair;
And if the earth-song has lost a tone,
The music of Heaven has sweeter grown.

But, Mother! albeit the coming years
Stretch away, away 'neath the clouds and tears,
An access of joy with thy grief is given—
Thou'rt mother now of a child in Heaven.

SUNLIGHT AND SHADOW.

How fitfully the sunlight and shadow chase each
other across the pathway of life ; now all hope, again
all cloud and darkness. Yesterday the whole world
seemed flooded with light. No cloud-dimmed rays
struggling through the mists of earth suggested a
thought of sorrow. Rivulets of pleasure seemed
sweeping outward to an ocean of joy. Hope gave
wing to imagination, while thought wandered far
away into the unexplored realm of the To-Come. O
bright yesterday ! Sweet respite from the realities of
life, how I love to recall thy fruition and thy promise!
Well is it for us that the heart has its resting places

along the highways, where it may gather strength for its course through the sands of the desert and the darkness of the valley, for we may be sure they stretch away in the distance. Ah! happy, happy yesterday, when song was on the lip, music in the heart!

But to-day—ah to-day! If there is song or music in the heart it is very sad. A shadow is resting there. The tardy light breaking through a leaden sky seems to reveal the clouds rather than the glories of the day. Hope has folded her wings and Memory wanders amid the shadowy and sorrowful paths of auld lang syne; for, strange as it may seem, we seldom live in the present. It is hope and memory—yesterday and to-morrow—that make up the sum of life, that fill our hearts and people our dreams, while to-day stands as a cipher on the dial of the years.

An undulating landscape of hill and valley, clear stream and muddy brook, ever reaches out toward the unexplored future, while a changeful sky of cloud and sunlight hangs over the present. Now we are rocked upon the bosom of the deep, while the angry storm sweeps around us; anon, the calm of a summer's morning embalms the spirits and rests like a benediction upon the life. In his "Dream Life" Mitchell beautifully says: "These cloud drifts float eternally, and eternally change their shapes upon the great over-arching sky of thought. You may seize the strong outlines which the passion breezes of to-day shall throw into their figures, but to-morrow may breed a whirlwind that will chase swift shadows over the heaven of your thought, and change the whole landscape of your life." And it is well. This constant drifting gives us glimpses of the cerulean sky that is ever bending above us, though often obscured; and permits us now and then to catch a vision of the jasper walls that rise beyond. In our fallen estate we cannot appreciate undimmed splendor, unbroken rest, constant calm, eternal peace. It is only the contrast that enables us to enjoy our blessings. Human nature becomes tired of inactivity, satiated with pleasure. One must be weary to enjoy rest, hungry to enjoy food—must have known sorrow to fully appreciate the quiet pleasures of life. And so we must not despair, even when enveloped in clouds. The sun shines brightly beyond and the clouds will lift "by and by." True, it may not be in this life; some of earth's children walk down to the brink of the River under the clouds, but we must know that He who "knoweth our frame" knoweth also what discipline is best for us, and that it is our Father's hand that is guiding us all the while. Vegetable life requires the darkness as well as the light, some forms of vegetation even developing best in shadowy places. In like manner there are those who develop best under the clouds of adversity, the full tide of prosperity tending to dwarf rather than promote that higher life into which it is His will we shall enter when we leave the chrysalis of clay through which we are developing for eternity. Then, welcome sunlight! welcome shadow! if they serve to bring us nearer Him who came to open a way through the drifting clouds of earth to the land where the shadows shall forever flee away—to the city whose "gates shall not be shut at all by day," "and there shall be no night there."

TO A SKEPTICAL STUDENT.

Knowledge, tho' grand, can never satisfy;
 But O! my doubting friend, there is a Power
Can lift thy aspirations to the sky,
 And give thee comfort in thy darkest hour.
And while thou drinks't of the "Pierian Spring"
 Which for thy thirsting MIND doth freely flow,
May thy immortal SPIRIT to HIM cling,
 . Whom it were highest wisdom thou shouldst know.

GETHSEMANE.

The heart hath its own Gethsemane,
   Where it boweth low in prayer;
And whether it find it soon or late,
   'Twill find it sometime, somewhere.

'Tis found in the way that leads to Christ,
   A garden, serene and still,
Where the soul must struggle as did its Lord,
   Ere to God it yields its will.

Aye, it lies just under the cross, where He
   Surrendered his life one day;
And all who enter the "Father's House"
   Must verily pass that way.

'Tis a lonely place; and each alone
   Must tread where its shadows lower;
In his agony even Jesus' friends
   Could not "watch with him one hour!"

Thy paths are safe, O, Gethsemane!
   And can never lead astray;
For whoso' walks with the Crucified
   Finds the Life, the Truth, the Way.

GATHER THEM IN.

[God has called scores upon scores of our noblest sons and daughters
to serve Him and spread abroad His blessed gospel in heathen lands, many
of whom are still with aching, longing hearts, and cannot go because we
have not furnished the means to send them.—REV. A. T. HAWTHORNE.]

Away in earth's wilderness, still, we are told,
There are thousands of children astray from the fold,
Exposed on the mountain to hunger and cold,
    Or athirst in the desert of Sin!
While God's own embassadors stand at our gate,
And for proper equipment most patiently wait—
Let us arm them in haste, lest they be too late
    To gather the little ones in.

Tho' the desert is lonely, the mountain so wild,
Their false show the dear children's feet have beguiled;
And yet there's no rest for the heart of a child
    On the mount, in the desert of Sin.
But, O, in the fold, with the tenderest care,
There is room for these lambs, there's food and to
    spare,
And the Good Shepherd's waiting to welcome them
    there—
    Let's send out and gather them in.

"TAKE NO THOUGHT FOR THE MORROW."

Oft there's song upon the lips or music in the heart
   That doth move in rythmic measure to a melan-
      choly air;
When, instead of notes of gladness,
There's a minor tone of sadness
   Floating round us and about us, and the world
      seems full of care.

And there's "sickness of the heart," born of the
      "hopes deferred,"
   Too subtle in the language of the earth to be
      express'd;
When a brooding on the morrow,
Half unconciously we borrow
   All the anguish of an evil that may never thrill
      the breast!

Oh! the weary, weary days, and the nights of
      wretchedness,
   When awake upon our pillow, back and forth we
      moan and toss;

The while our eyes grow tearful
And our spirit shrinks back, fearful
   Of the ghosts that haunt the bridges we may
     NEVER have to cross!

But methinks a lovely plain would e'er spread
     before our feet,
   If we would but heed this message—sweet and
     tender beyond price:
"Take no thought for the to-morrow,
['Tis the keynote of most sorrow,]
   Since "for each day the evil that it bringeth
     will suffice."

DAY DREAMS.

It is not without a purpose that the bright visions
which come to us in our realistic life are given.
Though they may be dispelled and we left to grope
our way in darkness, they lend us courage while they
last, and point us on toward the possibilities of the
future. It is the dreamer who succeeds in life. He
who has no aspiration beyond the present will never
obtain the goal made possible for him. It is he who

lets his dreams hover around the topmost round of the ladder, but is content to climb step by step, who makes the ascent complete. Should he look down from any other point, he becomes giddy, his body sways, and danger lurks about him; but when once his feet are firmly planted at the top; when once he takes in the exhilarating draught of the pure, serene atmosphere of success, he can calmly survey the conquered world at his feet. He sees the dangers through which he has passed, the difficulties he has surmounted, by ever having his eyes fixed at the top;—fixed on the zenith star of his ambition. It is this that has given him hope, and faith, and courage. True, the brightness of this star may sometimes have been obscured; but he knew the star was there; for, it is a fixed star, though he perchance was not in a position to bask in its beams. When we look out on the clear noon-day heavens, no stars are to be seen; but in the calm depths of some pure fountain we see their reflection; and we know the sky is not starless—our vision is simply finite.

Ah! truly our lives are rounded into completeness through the influence of our dreams. There come times when Faith seems dead, the star of Hope set; and our hands drop nerveless at our side. Suddenly, in the form of a day dream, a Bow of Promise spans our mental sky, and we rise above the clouded atmosphere that has surrounded us, to the clear heavens which encircle the world of Success, and with renewed courage, walk bravely on.

We are all dreamers. The gladsome smile breaking over the face of the little one upon its mother's knee, attests the fact that its infantile vision is reaching out into unseen vistas. The child has dreams of the unexplored realm of manhood or womanhood to which Hope lends many a brilliant hue. The old have dreams; but their dreams are of the past, over whose landscape sunshine and shadow have chased each other. Their memories are teeming with forms and faces, now chilled and faded by the blasts of life's autumn, or silently sleeping in some quiet Cave Hill or Greenwood The mind of the poet, the painter, or sculptor, is filled with beautiful pictures, such as the common eye may not look upon. The youth has dreams, when, stretched upon the grass beneath the foliage of some wide-spreading tree, on a summer's day, he looks far off into the fathomless depths of the bending heavens. Scenes of beauty, painted on a canvass of Hope's own creation, pass before his eyes. His mind, his heart, reaches onward.

Earth's music floats about him; and well it will be for him, if the sweet strains of hope and the gladsome notes of faith in the world, shall not be mellowed down by the touch of Time, and Memory yet stand out as the master-chord in the Harp of Life!

The maiden too has dreams. Seated upon a rustic seat, beside some beautiful stream, watching the dancing waves and drinking in their song, she sends forth her slight craft, full freighted with hope and faith, on the rippling waves of life's springtide, it may be to return a wreck, or laden with disappointments; for, while it is the dreamer who succeeds, we are far from saying that all dreams are fulfilled ; though full well we know that many a noble purpose, duly crowned, has been born of them.

These dreams are not to be despised. They are God-given and are meant for our good. They are ballast in the ship of Life, steadying it as it plows the turbulent waves of Time, and weighs anchor for the land of the Hereafter. But thousands of them, though beautiful they may be, are too etherial to be grasped by word or pen. The Poet-Priest of the South has beautifully said :

> "I have seen Thoughts in the Valley—
> Ah me! how my spirit was stirred!

And they wear holy veils on their faces,—
  Their footsteps can scarcely be heard;
They pass through the Valley, like Virgins,
  Too pure for the touch of a word."

These are bright meteors shooting across the sky of Thought, only to go out in darkness. But they are evidences of the Unseen; for, amid our dreams, there are longings and aspirations which we are conscious cannot be satisfied on earth. Aye, they give us glimpses of the attainable when mortality shall be merged into immortality. Rising above the material they grasp the immaterial, forming the link between the finite and the Infinite.

THE OTHER SIDE.

I tread, I tread life's way alone;
So many I have loved are gone,
The densest throng seems solitude,
And o'er me steals a pensive mood;
And sometimes as the daylight dies
Along the west in gentle sighs,
I hear still voices in the air,
And start—to find there's no one there.

Perhaps they float across the tide,
Across the tide so deep and wide,
From loved ones on the Other Side.

In gentle tones they come and go.
They come and go in rythmic flow;
As if the waves on shell-strewn beach
Had broken, broken into speech;
And tender as the breath of song,
The breath of song that glides along
Neath starlight, o'er the silvery tides,
As some light-winged gondola glides
'Twixt mimic shores on mimic seas,
Fanned by the soft caressing breeze;
And then before my vision glide
Forms that I know beyond the tide
Are resting on the Other Side.

On this side there remaineth four,
    But they are scattered far and wide;
Only one steps my threshold o'er
        At eventide, at eventide,
        As toward the west the shadows glide;
But He who sought his wandering sheep
O'er desert wastes, thro' waters deep,

Will keep my several ones in trust,
Untouched by sin, unstained by rust,
Until, (the waves of death defied)—
Beyond the tide, beyond the tide,
We'll gather on the Other Side.

SOMETIME.

What a goal in the future! How many dreams are to be realized, how many hopes to burst into full fruition, how many disappointments to meet with compensation, when we shall reach the enchanted realm of—Sometime! The way may be long and wearisome, our feet tired, our spirits flagging, but we are cheered by the anticipation of reaching this land which rises before our mental vision like the first clear view of one of 'the Islands of the Blest.

The little child, just starting out on life's pathway, asks you for something, and you tell him he shall have it, "Sometime." He wishes to know something more definite about the point around which his hopes are hereafter to center; and you mention the mile-posts, it may be of days, months or years, that he must pass before he shall reach that Sometime, that to him has become a desirable point; and he grows very impatient as the time slowly passes.

We all have glorious visions of things we shall have in the bright Sometime toward which we are traveling, and yet this wonderland of promise, whose fame is so widespread, like To-morrow, is undiscovered and unexplored, as far as we know. Many tell us they are seeking it, but none have returned to tell us about it; and we do know that vessels are often wrecked against the jagged rocks along its coasts.

I once saw a small pleasure boat gliding down a stream on a lovely summer's morning. The breath of flowers stole over the senses with soothing effect, while the glad strains of the woodland songsters floated across the waters from the overshadowing trees along the banks. The current was smooth, and the white sails flapped lazily in the soft breeze. There was something so intoxicating in the scene, the hour, and the undulating motions of the boat, that both officers and crew left their places and joined the passengers in their quiet and innocent games. But, as I had once sailed down that stream, I knew that, notwithstanding the present tranquillity, somewhere beneath the unruffled surface, Destruction lurked in waiting for all thoughtless ones who passed that way. However, there was a safe but narrow pass by which all danger could be avoided, and I gave those on board an anxious warning, at the same time pointing out the "pass." But the game was fascinating, and the players kept on, merely saying they saw no cause for alarm, but they would see about it—sometime. My heart grew heavy as I stood on the bank watching the boat now rapidly drifting beyond the reach of my warning voice. Presently, even startling me with its suddenness, for I could not exactly locate the danger once so narrowly escaped; there was a wild cry of distress, and a mad rushing and gurgling of waters, as the heedless boat was passing from sight; but above the sound of the dashing and foamy waves, there came on the wings of the wind the despairing cry, " We saw not our danger till it was too late—too late!"

We have all read of one distinguished for eloquence, learning and the force of his arguments, who once stood before a king and reasoned of "righteousness, temperance and a judgment to come;" and that as he reasoned the king trembled in his seat, so convinced was he of the importance of the subject; still, he sent the speaker away, saying he would call for him "at a more convenient season!" That "convenient season" is but another name for the "Sometime" which is never reached, but always recedes as we approach its supposed boundaries. O! if we would but realize that the past and future are alike beyond our reach, and that NOW is all we have, instead of staking our all upon hopes and dreams that can never be realized, because placed upon that alluring phantom—Sometime!

A great poet has said that "There is a tide in the affairs of men, which, taken at the flood, leads on to fortune." In like manner, there is a supreme moment in every life, which, improved, leads on to happiness. True, it may not be attained in this life; on the contrary, "it is written" that "In the world ye shall have tribulation;" but it will be in that country, of which it is said, "Eye hath not seen, nor ear heard, neither hath it entered into the heart of man to conceive of the joys" in store for those who may be accounted worthy to enter it.

"There comes an hour when all life's joys and pains
    To our raised vision seem
But as the flickering phantom that remains
    Of some dead midnight dream!

"There comes an hour when earth recedes so far,
  Its wasted, wavering ray,
Wanes to the ghostly pallor of a star
  Merged in the Milky-Way.

"Set on the sharp, sheer summit that divides
  Immortal Truth from mortal fantasie;
We hear the moaning of Time's muffled tides
  In measureless distance die!

"Past passions, loves, ambitions and despairs,
  Across the expiring swell,
Send thro' void space, like waves of Lethean airs,
  Vague voices of farewell.

"Ah, then! from life's long haunted dream we part,—
  Roused as a child new-born,
We feel the pulses of the eternal heart
  Throb thro' the eternal morn."

———

THE PASSING YEARS.

How rapidly the years are going past! It seems
but a little while since we paid the last tribute of respect to Eighty-nine, and lo! the solemn midnight
knell marks another era in our life, and reminds us
that another year has gone to join the centuries of
the past—the "years beyond the flood." And O how
silently it has passed! We see its traces all around

us, but we neither heard its footfall nor the rustle of its wings, as it hurried onward.

Many a ship that, full-freighted, was launched upon the bosom of the year Ninety has been wrecked, and gone down to rise no more. It has witnessed the overthrow of many ambitious desires, the death-throes of many joyous anticipations; has seen many lights extinguished, many stars set in darkness, and has looked on many new-made graves. But while it has left a scar on many a heart, a blight on many a life, a shadow on many a brow, and a vacant chair in many a home, its record has not all been sad. It has looked on many a birth, on many a wedding; has witnessed vows of fidelity consummated, the strengthening of weakened ties, the arousing of the latent energies of some who were on the brink of despair; has known many who were on the road to ruin reclaimed; and has seen the world of Science, Literature and Art take a pronounced step forward in the line of progress. And while the years go on, completing their cycles and marking their periods on the great dial of Time, these changes will go on, these transitions take place, these lights and shadows will succeed each other in the heart and in the life.

With each recurring year we turn the proverbial "new leaf," and set forward with the determination that the record shall be fair; and while we always fall short, we have the consolation of knowing that we have reached a higher plane in the moral world than we should have done had we set forward with no definite purpose in view. But our discomfiture often arises from the fact that Time is so silent in his movements, and we so prone to listlessness, that, ere we are aware, we are away down the stream, and many opportunities gone forever—our time beyond recovery: and the melancholy thought recurs to us that "Every moment lost on earth is echoed, 'lost,' in Heaven;" when, aroused to a sense of our heedlessness, we once more gird on our armor, and prepare for life's conflicts.

TO-MORROW.

I know of a land, not far away,
  Untrod by the foot of sorrow;
Amid whose forests the sunbeams play;
And its sands are laved by the tide of To-Day—
  Its magic name is—To-Morrow.

And fair it is as an Isle of the Blest,
　　With the blue sky bending over;
And glad expectancy thrills the breast
As we turn our eyes to the purpling west,
　　Its outlines to discover.

But we look in vain—tho' the rare perfume,　'
　　As our light bark skims the ocean,
Doth like the breath of Araby come
From the lovely land, each fragrant bloom
　　By the zephyrs set in motion.

Anon, drawing near the silvery strand,
　　We lean the low deck over,
And stretch a gladsome, welcoming hand,
Out tow'rd the wonderful sunlit land,
　　Round which our bright hopes hover.

And fain would we moor to some fair tree,
　　With its graceful boughs o'erbending;
Where the woodland songsters, blithe and free,
Their wildest, cheeriest minstrelsy,
　　With that of the waves is blending.

But alas! that we cannot gain the isle,
　　And o'er its bright paths wander!

Tho' its charming scenes the senses beguile,
As we near approach it recedes the while—
  A problem all may ponder.

O, is it a phantom, an idle dream,
  From fable-lore we borrow,
That the waves of To-Day which around us gleam
As they bear us on 'neath the sunset beam,
  Reach no country called To-Morrow?

Ah, no! 'Tis an isle in a boundless sea,
  Whose pleasures are supernal!
'Tis the name of the glorious land, where we
Shall enter the gates of the bright To Be,
  In the dawn of day eternal.

And now from these words of rhythm and rhyme,
  What lesson may we borrow?
Let's clasp to our breast this truth sublime—
By To-Day we measure the years of Time—
  Eternity, by To-Morrow.

SYMPATHY.*

I know thee not, O stranger! but thy words,
So full of sympathy and tender grace,
Come to my spirit like a healing balm,
And send a gladsome thrill along the veins.
Ev'n as the dewdrop to the dainty flower
That droops its petals 'neath the noontide sun,
The summer rain upon the thirsting earth,
Or kiss of zephyr on the aching brow,
So comes a kindly word from kindly lips.
And when, sometimes beneath the storm-racked sky,
Our life-boat glideth heavily amid
The foam-swept breakers and o'er bars of sand,
'Till we are fain to drop the useless oars,
'Tis sweet to know that, high above the wreck,
Earth holds one heart attuned to sympathy.

And as the rays of yonder crescent moon,
And the clear lustre of a myriad stars
Combine to chase away the clouds that hang
So darkingly above my hidden way—

*Reply to an anonymous letter expressing sympathy and encourage-
ment in my literary work.

As creeps miasma o'er a stagnant pool—
Thy dream-voice comes to my attentive ear;
And thro' the silent chambers of my heart
Sends music, sweet as fell from Orpheus' lyre,
When his soft fingers swept its vibrant strings
Amid the echoing hills of ancient Greece.
But sweet and wondrous as the strains must be
That thus could stay the river in its course
Toward the bosom of the beckoning deep;
Or tame the nature of the wildest beast
That roamed the pathless forest; or could cause
The loftiest tree to bow in silent awe,
Far sweeter are those wakened in the breast
Of earth's despondent ones, by sympathy.

And now, upon the earth which God hath made
So beautifully bright, there lives not one
So lowly that he may not send a gleam
Of light and joy across some shadowed path,
A note of music to some sorrowing heart;
Then simple tho' thy boon, my unknown friend,
Know thou that past the graceful tapestry
That veils my spirit from a careless world,
Thou'st touched a chord that softly echoes back
The tender tribute of a grateful heart.

THE JEWS.

No people on earth can claim a purer origin than the Jews. They are direct descendants of the "child of promise," the great antitype of the promised Messiah, and have from the days of Abraham been "a peculiar people," mingling little with the people of other nationalities either by marriage or association. Hence the conclusion that, notwithstanding the deep-seated prejudice existing in the world against them, no purer blood flows through human veins than flows through theirs. It was of this line came all the grand old Bible characters whom we most revere and love—patriarchs, and prophets, and kings, and priests, and John the Baptist, and Jesus of Nazareth and his disciples. And yet the mind of the Gentile race has always been prejudiced against them. Early prejudice we know has much to do with our later estimate of things, and often prevents our giving due weight to facts. We take a position between facts and preconceived opinions, and are unwilling, or have not the moral courage, even in the face of testimony, to abandon our strongholds. It would require deep research to enable us to give all the grounds of this prejudice whose existence we accept as a fact. In the divine economy it is doubtless a part of the discipline which God will overrule for our good and—theirs. It will be remembered that when David fled before the face of Absalom, Shimei, of the house of Saul, came out and cursed him and threw stones at him ; and that when Abishai, the nephew of David and brother of Joab, in his righteous indignation, would have slain Shimei, the king said, " Let him curse, because the Lord hath said unto him 'Curse David.' " Of this prejudice the most we can say is that God permits it.

About two thousand years before the dawn of the Christian era, Abraham emigrated from Mesopotamia, the Padan Aram of Genesis, to the west side of the Euphrates, and settled in Palestine, from which circumstance his descendants were known as Hebrews ; the word signifying "from beyond the Euphrates." It was not until after their return from their captivity in Babylon that they were known among other nations as Jews, this appellation being derived from the word Judea, the Roman name of the most southern of the three divisions of Palestine.

But Abraham did not at this time possess the

land—it was still but the "promised land;" for we are told that "By faith Abraham, when he was called to go out into a place which he should AFTER receive as an inheritance, obeyed; and he went out, not knowing whither he went. By faith he sojourned in the land of promise as in a strange country, dwelling in tents with Isaac and Jacob, heirs with him of the same promise." From this Scripture we learn what has been stated,—that Abraham's inheritence was still prospective. It was not until after their deliverance from their four hundred years of Egyptian bondage that his descendants, having subdued the Canaanites, took formal possession of the promised inheritance. Later, on account of continued disobedience, they temporarily forfeited their rights, and were carried to Babylon. For seventy years they remained captive in this strange land. But they did not forget Jerusalem. Among the hills and plains of Palestine were home and freedom; and "they hung their harps on the willows," and refused "to sing the Lord's songs in a strange land." And the God of Abraham heard the cry of the contrite heart, and a second time delivered them from bondage. But alas! they are now for the third time in bondage; not to Egypt or Babylon, not for four hundred or for seventy years;

but for eighteen centuries they have been scattered abroad, having no heritage among the nations of the earth. By rejecting Him whom God had sent, they forfeited their birthright, and are in exile, where they will remain till the Gentile nations shall have received the gospel, when the "blindness in part" that has "happened to Israel till the fullness of the Gentiles shall be come in," shall be removed, and they too will accept Christ, and his saying shall again be verified, that "the last shall be first and the first last;" and for the third time—the mystic number of the Scriptures—they shall be restored to their inheritance.

In their exile they have not been permitted for the most part to enjoy the rights and privileges usually accorded to strangers or aliens. Even Christianity, whose very spirit is that of religious toleration, has been intolerant of this people. Imperial edicts and ecclesiastical decrees have been rigorous as regarded them. But, notwithstanding they have been persecuted, oppressed, enslaved, degraded, and expelled from different countries, they stand before us to-day as living witnesses of the fact that no power on earth is able to destroy the people whom God chose in Abraham. With the increasing light of Christianity their condition has been greatly ameliorated. From

the days of Cromwell their privileges as citizens
of England were gradually extended until in 1858
the climax of toleration was reached by their being
made eligible to admission into the English Parlia-
ment.   In our own country they have perfect liberty.

As to learning, no people has advantage of the
Jews.   They stand in the front ranks of intellectual
advancement, both in science and general literature.
The larger proportion of the professors of German
universities and academies is Jews.   A trustworthy
authority has said that the Jews are "by the unani-
mous verdict of the historians and philosophers of
the present time reckoned among the chief promoters
of humanity and civilization."   Much might be said
of their advancement in the fine arts, music, painting
and the drama; as many Jewish names are familiar
to our ears in connection with these, but we must desist.   We are only astonished at what has been attained in these things by a people in exile—a people
in whom the prophetic words of Jesus when he wept
over Jerusalem, have been so terribly fulfilled.   A
quotation from an eminent writer of their own race
will give a vivid word-picture of what they have en-
dured: "If there is a gradation in sufferings, Israel
has reached the highest acme; if the long duration of

sufferings, and the patience with which they are borne, ennobles, the Jews defy the high-born of all countries ; if a literature is called rich which contains a few classical dramas, what place deserves a tragedy lasting a millennium and a half, composed and enacted by the heroes themselves !"

But as of old, in the days of their Babylonian captivity, the faces of the Jews are toward Jerusalem, where, it is said, their numbers are increasing. Because they "knew not the day of their visitation," they have been temporarily deposed; but we believe the hour of deliverance is drawing near when they will not only come again into the possession of their earthly inheritance, but will be restored to their position as God's "peculiar people " in the original sense as typical of the children of faith ; and that in that day the voices of Jew and Gentile will unite in the gladsome strain, "The Lord God Omnipotent reigneth !" Their own faith in their final restoration has never wavered, and this faith has seemed to be emphasized with a substantial foundation since Rothschilds has held a mortgage on Palestine—the land that has witnessed the most wonderful manifestations of God's presence—the land consecrated by the footprints of the world's Redeemer.

GOOD NIGHT.

Alone, alone in the old house, dear;
My loved ones scattered—some far, some near;
Some resting where, 'neath the open sky,
The leaves breathe a dirge as the winds pass by;
And when the beautiful day goes down,
And night comes on, with its star-set crown,
Of all who gave to my world its light,
There's no one left me to say, " Good night."

Alone, alone in the old house, dear;
The morning of life with its hope and cheer,
And its noontide glory, so long passed o'er,
That shadows are gathering around my door;
And the silence, deep'ning the air of gloom
That hovers about each vacant room,
Remains unbroken by footstep light,
By child-caress or the fond " Good night."

Alone, alone in the old house, dear,
Only God and the angels near,
When I lift to Heaven my prayer or hymn
At morning, or when the day grows dim ;

And if the Messenger—sent to all— .
At the dear old house some day should call,
And bear me up to the Hills of Light,
There's no one to kiss me and say, " Good night."

Alone, alone in the old house, dear;
But, above its silence and gloom, I hear
A low voice saying, within my breast,
" Thou'rt nearing the borderland of rest ;"
And then I remember with grateful prayer,
'Tis written, " There shall be no night there ;"
So, passing from darkness into light,
With joy I shall bid the world " Good night."

OMISSION.

Neglected duties are the ghosts
    That haunt us thro' the years;
The specters that e'er fill the breast
    With unavailing fears.

'Tis not the yielding to a wrong
    That, at the set of sun,
Brings to the conscience such remorse
    As duties left undone.

The kindly word we might have said,
The smile we might have given,
But did not, prove, alas, at night,
A veil 'twixt us and Heaven.

THE POET'S HERITAGE.

"Sing, Poet, sing!"   The universe is thine !
The lofty mountain and the shady dell,
The roaring cataract, the purling brook,
The moon, with her bright retinue of stars,
And night and morn, and noon, and tearful eve,
And death, and hell, and even Heaven itself,
Are truly thine if thou art poet true—
The called and set apart by seal divine
To wake the silent strings of sacred lyre ;
And that is sacred lyre which doth give
The ever-varied yet harmonious notes
Of truth and beauty.

Brightest visions pass
In stately train before the poet's eyes,
Unseen by others howsoever versed
In ancient lores or new philosophies.
These may pertain to earth's or heaven's laws;

Those to the dreams and vagaries of men,
Who walked with Plato 'neath the plane-trees' shade
In academic gardens. But, alike,
The fairest dream and grandest theory,
Must perish with the things consigned to dust,
Not founded on the solid rock of Truth.

The Poet is the prophet of his time.
In the still watches of the midnight hour,
When Death's twin-brother holds all life at bay,
And benedictions rest upon the world,
His ever-wakeful and far-grasping mind,
From the deep-graven record of the past,
Gleans subtler meaning than is wont to lie
Upon the surface of events exposed;
And from its hidden meaning gains a clue,
Which, winding thro' a gloomy maze of doubt,
Opens at last upon an eminence,
With air so pure the mists lift from the eyes,
And, far away, in undulating waves,
Stretches the landscape of Futurity.

Lightly he treads this great highway of Thought,
And, from his dizzy height beholding, far
Along the plain of unborn years, the scenes
To be enacted on the boards of time,

Freighted with prophecy, he launches forth
His weirdly-graceful argosy of song.

And be he infidel or man of faith,
The rounded numbers of his verse will take
Undying forms of loveliness and truth.
When wicked Balaam to his aid had called
The son of Beor to pronounce a curse
On Israel, the chosen of the Lord,
A blessing, not a curse, escaped his lips.
Thus : " God is not a man that he should lie,
Nor son of man that he should e'er repent.
How then curse him whom God hath never cursed,
Or how defy whom He hath not defied ?"
"How goodly are thy tents, O Israel !
How fair thy gardens by the river's side,
Where the lign-aloes which the Lord hath set,
And lordly cedars cast a grateful shade."

And there was one even in our modern time
Of wayward mood and unbelieving heart,
Whose song was eloquent with prophecy;
The wandering cloud became a stepping-stone
From which he looked upon the universe,
The while he clothed in songful phrase some thought
Caught from the bosom of infinity.

There is a sweetness and a joy in song,
Which only poets feel.   Unknown to fame
Is many a bard whose songs shall swell
Amid the arches of eternity,
That on the earth fell on unheeding ears;
For what is true is truly never lost.
When Time himself, grown old, shall fold his hands
And sink into the tomb of Nothingness;
And stars, waxed pale beneath the brighter beams
Of the Eternal Morn, shall pass away,
Dissolved like vapors of the summer night;
And the fair moon shall dim, whose tender light
Is but a reflex of the Day-god's face,
Then shall the Poet in his native realm
Take up the soulful strain broken by death
And send it trilling down the deathless years.

THREESCORE AND TEN.

What radiant dreams visit the heart, when, in the
freshness of life's fair morning, we look out on the
beautiful vistas that stretch along the journey ordi-
narily allotted to man—our threescore and ten years.
True, this is an infinity which our minds cannot

grasp. The few years that we have passed, though bright, so bright, have seemed long; for the siren, Hope, pictures the future as brighter still, and so our aspirations lead us on; and, all unheeding the beauty and fragrance along our pathway, we look forward to, it may be, an unattainable good. We do not think of death. The infant, the merry child, the gladsome maiden, the buoyant youth, may go from our side down to the quiet grave to sleep "under the daisies," but the life-current dances too joyously along our veins to think of death—for us surely the end is not yet; and so, neglecting these words of the wise man, "Remember now thy Creator in the days of thy youth, while the evil days come not, nor the years draw nigh when thou shalt say I have no pleasure in them," we go recklessly on, at last, perhaps, to wreck our life hopes on the turbulent bosom of that awful gulf, Too Late.

But a brighter picture comes before us—a beautiful, mild, serene old age. Such an example we have in our midst. On Thursday, November 24, Rev. J. N. Lewis, the venerable pastor of the Presbyterian churches of Milton and Bagdad, closed the record of his threescore and twelve years. His snowy hair tells us that the winters have not gone by unmarked, but

the genial smile that so often plays about his face
breathes of the summer within. And O, what changes
he has seen by the way on his long journey! What
dreams have been dispelled, what few hopes realized!
He has seen the fields whitening for harvest, while
youthful ministers have been called, perhaps, from
his side, to lay down the sickle. He has seen the
Church move forward, and the missionary spirit
deepening and widening in its influence until it em-
braces the very Isles of the Sea; for though Ignorance asserts that the Religious World has a retro-
grade motion, persons who keep up with the history
of Christian progress know differently. Religion
may seem to stand still sometimes; but it is only
seeming—it is simply gathering strength for a fiercer
conflict—a conflict that may shake empires and kingdoms. Listen to Disraeli on this point :

"Wiseacres go on talking about the decline of
religion, and meanwhile religion goes on building up
and tearing down empires. Religion dying in the
world! And yet if you touch religion, or tread on
religious convictions, a revolution will be kindled in
twenty-four hours in any Nation in Christendom as
fierce as that which deluged France with blood ninety
years ago."

The sin of a people may prove their salvation—the turning point in their history; their burdened conscience may become too heavy to bear, and their very wrath may be turned to the praise of God. Doubtless our reverend friend has noticed these things with deep interest. But he has borne the heat and burden of the day; and the time of his departure is drawing near, when, we doubt not, in the language of the great Apostle, he can say, " I have fought a good fight; I have finished my course, I have kept the faith; henceforth there is laid up for me a crown of righteousness, which the Lord, the righteous judge, will give me in that day." At farthest, it cannot be long ere the ministerial mantle shall fall from his shoulders, but, alas! where among us can be found an Elisha—one worthy to take it up ?

It is certainly a glorious privilege to the weary laborer of almost three-fourths of a century to see the world, with its sorrows, its doubts, and its shadows, receding, while the domes and spires of the New Jerusalem loom up across the River. Though it is appointed unto man once to die, methinks there is beauty and inspiration in the thought of being almost Home.

MUSIC.

Born of the deepest, the brightest, the best,
And a feeling by mortal tongue never exprest,
Than Music there's nothing diviner been giv'n
To cheer man on earth, or allure him to Heav'n.

On light, viewless wings, we escape thro' its bars,
And soar far away 'cross the path of the stars;
Till our feet press the highway of infinite spheres,
Where no calendar's kept of the seasons and years.

O, the Spirit of Song! with its wonderful chords—
Too light and ethereal to wed unto words;
It stirs the soul's depths, like a fathoming rod—
Wakes echoes erst sacred to Silence and God.

When the earth, like a wand'rer, escaping the storm,
Out of darkness and shadows of Chaos took form;
The stars of the Morning, the unnumber'd throng
That encircle the Throne, told their gladness in song.

A dialect here, 'tis the language of Heaven;
And much of the sweetness celestial is given
To those who will cherish the gift so sublime
That lifts them away from the sorrows of time.

DIVIDED BUT TRUE.

I think of thee loved one! At evening's calm hour.
  As day slowly glides thro' the doors of the west,
And gentle winds sigh in the vine-trellised bower,
  A sweet thought of thee steals over my breast.

And when neath the burdens of care I am bowed,
  And the sparkle and foam melt away from life's
      wine
And shadows like twilight my spirit enshroud,
  The tendrils of thought still around thee entwine.

Aye, often in fancy I see thy fair face,
  And eyes whose expression I ne'er can forget,
And with pencil, inspired by affection, I trace
  Thy features—so dear to my memory yet.

How sacred our love! all undimmed by the years,
  With their close-tangled network of shadow and
      sheen ;
Tho' Fate hath divided us wide as the spheres,
  Hope, charity, faith, keep our bosoms serene.

COME UNTO ME.

[Suggested by a sermon of Rev. R. T. Hanks while pastor of the First Baptist Church, Dallas, preached from the words: "Come unto me all ye that labor," etc.]

" Come unto Me !" So soft and low
These words of invitation flow,
To weary hearts from lips divine,
Who can the dear request decline ?

" Come unto Me !"   How passing sweet
To lay our burden at His feet,
And in our erstwhile troubled breast
Find the blest calm of perfect rest.

" Come unto Me !"   An answering chord
Thrills in my bosom at the word,
And my tired heart, so prone to roam,
With trembling faith replies " I come !"

"Come unto Me !"   O sacred Guest
Of earth !—come at thine own behest;
From all earth's idols set me free,
Nor let me turn again from Thee.

DUTIES.

Sometimes along lief's pathway we reach a point where we think to lay aside our burdens; and our hearts beat with exultation in the light of the prospective liberty; while far away in the distance stretches a smooth plain, set with trees and dotted with flowers; only disappearing where the Seen is merged into the Unseen. It may be that light clouds are floating overhead, and dim shadows falling at our feet; still, all is peaceful, and there is a restful feeling in the prospect. But alas! the inexorable law of Necessity too soon awakens us from our dreams, and reminds us that our labors are not done; while rising superior to this law we hear a gentle voice saying, "Work while it is called to-day for the night cometh when no man can work;" and once more taking up our burdens we address ourselves to our task, feeling that if Adam in his sinless estate was not exempt from toil, it is but meet that we, his degenerate children, should labor in our respective fields until the Master shall bid us lay down our implements of toil and rest.

It may be that the dreams of ambition, which once nerved us with strength and energy for hard conflicts in the battle of life, have faded, as all dreams must fade as the hopes that brighten them disappear; and that life's firmament has become perceptibly dimmed. It matters not. Necessity admits of no apology—will hear no excuse. But there is this consolation, that as Necessity is the mother of Invention, she often improvises weapons adapted to our peculiar circumstances, with which we go forth fully equipped for every emergency, and ready to meet the conflicts of a world on which we had turned our backs so resignedly !

It is with something of this feeling that we enter upon the duties and responsibilities of the new year. We find that each recurring week, month and year, brings its own duties, labors and responsibilities, and, shrinking from them, we only burden our consciences; for while the race is not always to the swift nor the battle to the strong, a clear conscience, a light heart, a soft pillow and refreshing slumber, are the natural results of duties well performed, though our efforts seem to prove a failure. Perhaps the hearts of some who glance over these pages will echo our sentiment and follow our thought. To such we extend a kindly

New Year's greeting. The great heart of humanity
responds to one chord—that of sympathy. What
dew is to the flower, sympathy is to the heart; and,
scattered along the highways and byways of life the
good it does cannot be estimated. The consciousness
of awakening a responsive thrill in other breasts
sometimes arouses us to renewed efforts when we are
almost ready to falter :

> " For a very struggle at best is life;
>   If we knew the struggle along the line
>   We should shrink to accept this gift divine.
>
> "Sometimes, in the hush of the evening hour,
>   We think of the leisure we meant to gain,
>   And the work we would do with the hand and brain.
> ' I am tired to-night, I am lacking power
>   To think,' we say; 'I must wa t until
>   My brain is rested and pulse is still.'
>
> " O woman and man! There is never rest;
>   Dream not of leisure that will not come
>   Till age shall make you both blind and dumb.
> You must live each day at your very best ;
>   The work of the world is done by few—
>   ` God asks that a part be done by you.
>
> " Say oft of the years as they pass from sight,
>   This, this is life with its golden store,
>   I shall have it once but it comes no more.
> Have a purpose and do it with your might;
>   You will finish your work on the Other side,
>   And heart and brain will be satisfied."

THE TWO ANGELS.

A PERSIAN LEGEND.

There are two angels by us, day and night,
Standing on either side.   One on the right
  Notes every cheerful word and tender thought
  And kindly labor, by the fingers wrought,
And writes in a book with pen of gold ;
  While on the left the sister-angel stands
  With face averted, and with trembling hands
Each evil deed upon a scroll records
And wicked thought that blossoms into words;
  Then, with the patience born of pity, waits
  With anxious face before the Ivory Gates,
To blot it out as Allah gives the power,
Repentance coming ere the midnight hour ;
If not, to pass it in as 'twas enrolled.

BLIND.

"If I had known !"   Ah me !   If I had known,
  The day thou questionedst me what now I know,
  I might have won thee to avert the blow,
  Which in the dust of anguish laid thee low ;

Even tho' I must have sacrificed my own
    Most blissful dream, and that of one I love,
    To turn thee from a pathway time doth prove,
Was full of snares for thy unwitting feet,
Ambushed 'mid flowers with dews of morning sweet;
    But such was not to be, dear one, and so
    Along rough ways thy bruised feet must go,
    With none but me to understand and know;
While I o'er life's Sahara walk alone
A path I had not trod—if I had known.

MAY.

Queen of months, with chaplet gay,
After April comes the May,
    With the breath of Flora sweet;
Flower by flower and leaf by leaf
For a gladsome reign, tho' brief,
    April weaves a crown complete
    For the maid of dainty feet—
For the queen that cometh after
Radiant with song and laughter,
    Then the Nymph of smiles and tears
    Joins the children of dead years.
Queen of months, in bright array,
After April comes the May.

NO HOME ON EARTH.

Our citizenship is in Heaven.—[PAUL.

There is a magic in that little word:
It is a mystic circle that surrounds
Comforts and virtues never known beyond
Its hallowed limits. Oftimes at eve
Amid my wanderings I have seen far off
The lonely height which spake of comfort there.
It told my heart of many a joy of home—
And my poor heart was sad. When I have gazed
From some high eminence on goodly vales,
And cots and villages embowered below,
The thought would rise that all to me was strange
Amid the scene so fair; nor one small spot
Where my tired heart might rest and call it Home.
—[SOUTHEY.

The months and years as they go by only serve
to verify the words of the great apostle, that "we
have no abiding city here." Truly, we are pilgrims
and sojourners. The places that we designate with
the sacred name of home are simply way-stations
along the road of life, where we rest for a time under
our "own vine and fig tree;" ever conscious that we
may at any time be called to take up our pilgrim-
staff and journey on. Many such places mark the
path we have already traversed, and many fond
memories are associated with them ; but we are learn-

ing not to "set our affections" upon these things, but to bury them with other memories, under the dead leaves of a receding past, and to set our faces onward.

Just now there rises before me the vision of a beautiful "dream-home," situated far across the flower carpeted prairies of Texas, at the foot of a long range of mountains. A fountain of water, clear as crystal, rippling up from beneath a rocky bed, sparkles and dances in the bright beams of the morning sun, as they penetrate the graceful foliage of overshadowing trees. Here, on a golden summer day of the long ago, when hope stood sentinel along our way, we paused and planned a home. But alas! it never arose above the ideal—the "castle in the air." Scarcely had the first stake been set which gave it a stamp of the real, when we were called to gird on our sandals and prepare for journeying. Ah! life is indeed a scene of unfinished designs. Verily, a "man deviseth his ways, but the Lord directeth his steps." After as manifold wanderings as characterized the progress of the children of Israel through the wilderness, we at last pitched our tent in Florida, the land of sunshine and tropical beauty, and once more set up our Lares and Penates and dared give it the name of Home.

Here we expected to spend the afternoon and evening of life amid pleasant and familiar surroundings ; and when at last the "appointed time" should come, to step on board the palace car bound for the eternal city—"the city which hath foundations, whose builder and maker is God." But again there came a summons, signed and sealed by the unerring hands of Providence, to strike our tents once more, and, like Abraham, go forth not knowing whither we went ; and for the last time, it may be, we have looked upon those beloved scenes and surroundings which we had grown accustomed to call our own ; for the last time gazed upon the beautiful trees beneath whose shadows we hoped to rest when life's sun should decline westward ; and caught glimpses of the lovely bay,

> Whose waters, by the light winds kissed,
> Sparkled and glowed like amethyst.

And for the last time looked on the bright roses and lilies planted by loving hands, which, frail and tender, are already folded in the sweet sleep which "He giveth His beloved"—lovely plants whose burden of blooms was to lend fragrance and beauty to this last station along the railway of the years.

For the last time! What sadness, what pathos, linger about these simple words. It sends a thrill to the heart to part with even a casual acquaintance, or an object of indifference, haunted by the thought that it is for the last time; but when the acquaintance is a dear friend, and the object one associated with a beloved home, how infinitely sadder is it to feel " that we shall see their face no more."

O ye changing scenes of time when will ye give place to the unchangeable? So many are the vicissitudes of this life that we are ready at times to say as did the patriarch of old: "Few and evil have the days of the years of my life been, though they have not attained to the days of the years of the life of my fathers' in the days of their pilgrimage." Sometimes, too, we tire of the fare at these stations and long to partake of the fruit of the Tree of Life, and to drink of the fountain that flows from beneath the throne in that kingdom in which are concentrated all the sweetest names known to mortal tongue—Mother, Father, Jesus, Heaven, Home.

THE WITHERED FLOWER.

Mother, thy blossom is not dead,
　Tho' withering it lies ;
Exotic, God transplanted it
　To bloom in Paradise.

Too fragile for our rugged clime,
　To cheer thy heart 'twas given,
Then claimed, to draw thy thoughts from earth
　And center·them in Heaven.

Tho' brief its stay, it brought to thee
　A blessing from above ;
It touched the joysprings of thy heart
　And waked new chords of love.

And while thou feel'st that something bright
　Is from thy pathway gone ;
There's comfort in the glorious thought,
　That it is still thine own.

Like thee, I miss a lovely flower,
　Transferred from earthly blight ;
But we will claim our blossoms when
　We tread the Fields of Light.

MUSINGS.

If over the shadowy bridge of Death
Our friends could recross the Jordan's tide,
   With the same sweet voice, the tender smile,
   And walk with us for a little while,
As in the days vanished, side by side;
   With all they have seen and felt and know,
   Of things not "lawful" for them to show,
   Do you really think we could wish it so ?

Ah ! nevermore could they seem the same,
Who have walked with Jesus the streets of gold;
   Who've caught the fragrance of that bright sphere,
   Where summertime lasts thro' all the year—
This life to them were "a tale that's told ;"
   And we could never commune again
   Of common sorrows and joys, as when
   They knew no paths but the paths of men.

"The Lord knows best," we are wont to say,
And seemingly bow to His gracious will ;
   But in the deep silence of the soul,
   Scarce understood and beyond control,
Somewhat of rebellion lingers still ;

For the way seems barren—we miss them so,
Wherever we turn, wherever we go,
Who have shared our pleasures and cares below.

I know 'tis best we cannot recall
Those who have crossed to the farther shore;
And the beautiful promise thrills our breast,
That for us "remains" also, that "rest"
When the farewells and partings of earth are o'er;
And time doth soften the deepest grief,
And afterwhile there will come relief,
For the longest path of life is brief.

MISSIONS.

How a Christian in the nineteenth century can be opposed to either home or foreign missions is in-comprehensible, with the work of the great Exemplar of Christianity before us as given in the gospel. In His teachings and ministrations to His own people, Jesus illustrated the work of the home missions; and that of the foreign, when he went into the coasts of Tyre and Sidon and healed the daughter of the Canaanitish woman of whom He declared that He had not found so great faith, "No, not in Israel." The same faith and zeal is characteristic of foreign nations when they receive the gospel at the present time. Not long since I was reading a short sketch of one of the mission stations in Mexico. The people who had received the word gladly were very poor, but so impressed were they with the importance of sending the gospel to others, that they gave of their low wages until the missionary had to compel them to desist. They had the spirit of the primitive Christians upon them. A similar report comes from other foreign fields, while we who were nursed in the very lap of the gospel, alas, give so grudgingly. Ah! if we would only think.

The importance of this work is impressed upon every page of the New Testament. Methinks the great mission field was in the mind of God, with His Son to institute the work, when the first promise was made, that the "seed of the woman should bruise the serpent's head." And then before Jesus left the courts of light to enter upon His work, as if to comfort Him in view of the great sacrifice He was about to make for a lost world, the Father said to Him :

"Ask of me and I shall give thee the heathen for thine inheritance, and the uttermost part of the earth for thy possession." Eighteen hundred and fifty-nine years have measured their revolutions upon the dial of time since the redemption price was paid, and the cry, " It is finished !" announced to man that the last link in the chain which bound him to the Law was broken. Forty-three days later the risen Redeemer, having led his disciples out as far as Bethany, blessed them and said : "Go ye into all the world and preach the gospel to every creature." Thus we see how tenderly he carried the heathen upon his heart. His last thoughts were given to them. And yet how feebly we follow His example, how little thought we give to that which burdened his heart. "Into all the world" has been sounding down the years for more than eighteen centuries with a force that should startle the listless Christian ; for its import is simply that nations are sitting in the region and shadow of death, because they have not received the light the apostles were commanded to bear to them. And why have they not ? Alas ! that it should be said that it is on account of the indifference of Christians ; that while the eternal destinies of nations are hanging on our work, self is engrossing our time and we are "spending money for that which is not bread, and labor for that which satisfieth not," building up names or

reputations we hope will live after us, not remembering that these are of a perishable nature and may go
down with the first breath of adversity, while the
character that is to be tested by the light of the Last
Day is being neglected. Could we but keep before
our minds the thought of the tenderness of Jesus toward the heathens, we could never become indifferent.
Not content with the commission given to His disciples as he was about to ascend to Heaven, a half
century later he returned to earth, and appearing to
the "beloved disciple" on the isle of Patmos, sent another broad and beautiful invitation to the world, a
clause of which reads, "And let him that heareth say,
Come." Truly, if our hearts were just right, we
would be forwarding this invitation to those who
have not heard it. Or could we stand upon the summit of the spiritual Nebo and catch a glimpse of the
Land of Promise, feeling conscious that our inheritance lies over there ; then turn, and with a sweep of
the landscape, take in the nations perishing in idolatry for want of the bread of life which God has placed
in our hands, bidding us scatter it abroad, methinks
the talk about not believing in foreign missions would
be blotted from our creed forever, and we would be
ready to give more time and money to this work.

The cry of "the heathen at home needing the gospel" is a weapon used simply to ward off from our purses the claims of foreign missions; and those who use it with most ease have another, "Charity begins at home," with which they are equally skilled when home missions present their claims. In the hearts of those who resort to these weapons there is no room for the heathen. As far as they are concerned those who sit in the shadow of idolatry may go down in darkness. But I am glad to know that the whole Christian world is awakening to the importance of foreign missionary work. Every true believer in the Bible has been confident that such a time would come, though, through our indifference it has doubtless been delayed.

But we have His word that "not a jot or tittle shall pass from the law till all be fulfilled." And Isaiah, looking with prophetic vision down the long line of years, and seeing the fulfillment of the promise, elsewhere quoted, which was made to the Son, was constrained to exclaim, "He shall see of the travail of his soul and be satisfied." This result is being brought about alone through the instrumentality of Christians; and I thank God that He has given to the church men and women who are willing

to consecrate time, money and talent to the work of
hastening the accomplishment of the time when "a
nation shall be born in a day." The fruit of their
labors is being gathered into sheaves ready for garner-
ing. But the field is large and the laborers few;
therefore, with our purses in our hands, let us "pray
the Lord of the harvest that he will send forth more
laborers into the harvest."

OUR MODERN D. D'S.

Alas, alas that the Pulpit
    Should be filled with great D. D.'s!
Not once do the holy Scriptures
    Refer to a class like these;
Who stand in the pride and glory
    Bestowed by a human power,
In the van of competition
    For the honors of life's hour.

For how can the worldly preacher,
    Thus seeking for worldly fame,
Tell of the "meek and lowly"
    With these affixed to his name?

How point the way he pointed
  Thro' the straight and narrow gate,
With name and heart o'erburden'd
  With such unhallowed weight ?

Elijah, Moses and David,
  Each with his simple name,
Attained the loftiest summit
  Yet known to the world of fame ;
And Paul, the grandest preacher
  Whose name in The Word we meet,
Gathered rich jewels of wisdom,
  Low at Gamaliel's feet.

Yet never did this vain title
  Salute his consecrate ears,
Albeit his fame has been spreading
  Along the succeeding years,
Till there is no nation or kindred,
  Or island in all the seas,
To which it has not been wafted
  On wings of the generous breeze.

D. D. or doctor ! a teacher—
  A teacher of things divine !

Alas, how few can this honor,
   Or semblance of honor decline!
And yet 'twould seem when the Master
   Hath called his servant by name,
He hath surely lifted him upward
   To the highest heights of fame.

Besides, there's never a sentence
   In all God's beautiful word,
To justify such assumption,
   In the followers (?) of our Lord ;
Instead, on the sacred pages,
   Where the "old, old story" is told,
" Be not conformed" is written
   In letters of purest gold.

D. D. or doctor!   How coldly
   It falls from a brother's lips,
When the beauty of life is hidden
   Neath Fortune's sudden eclipse ;
When the wings of Faith are lifting,
   And Hope from the bosom flees,
How vain seems the worldy title
   As expressed in these D. D's !

But, Brother !   That thrills the bosom,
  Calms the deep sea of unrest,
And stirs the tenderest emotions
  That live in the human breast;
And points to that Elder Brother,
  Who hunger'd and wept and died,
And draws us nearer each other,
  And Him, the crucified.

O preacher ! wouldst thou be useful,
  Clasp this message to thy heart—
No power can confer an honor,
  On the one God sets apart ;
But the souls he wins for Jesus
  Along his appointed way,
Shall be his crown of rejoicing
  In the great " Crowning Day."

PULPIT AND PEW.

[The following lines were written in reply to the above poem,
" Our Modern D.-D's."]

Alas, that the pew should hold up to view
  The foibles and faults of the preachers!
The pew ought to know that titles and show
  Are to meet the demand of its creatures.

A preacher may be, sans college degree,
 Instructive to saint and to sinner;
The wide gaping pew shows learning can do
 But little as an audience winner.

Tho' prudent and holy, he succeeds but slowly,
 With no D. D. to swell on the eye;
Even those that deride these tokens of pride,
 Will let him in solitude die.

It is vain to contrast the now with the past,
 And tell us of David and Paul;
The pews of those days made no such displays
 Of pride as now greet us all.

Those that sat in the pew, dressed not as they do
 Now in gems and in silks that rustle;
With headgear and a' that yclept bonnet or hat,
 High-heeled shoes and overgrown bustle.

Not with silver and gold were they tricked out of old,
 With coiffure and costly apparel;
Steel hoops were unknown and no dresses were shown
 Bulging out like the sides of a barrel.

Then the pew worshipped God more than money and sod—
 Yea, they worshiped in truth and in spirit;
Preachers then preached the word and truth only was heard,
 Because people assembled to hear it.

Now 'tis different far, some first-magnitude star
 Alone in the pulpit can stand;
The pompous D. D., as the teacher we see
 In response to the churches' demand.

Were St. Paul now alive, scant support he'd derive
    From the fashion filled pews of to-day;
Were the truth simply told, as it was once, of old,
    Not e'en the church member would stay.
              —[W. H. B., of Denton, Texas.

O, W. H. B.! Methinks I can see
At the end of thy name that "pompous D. D.!"
Or thou never had'st tried to excuse all the pride
To that useless title so nearly allied !

'Till now I ne'er knew that the minister true
Was rigged out in titles to "draw" for the pew !
Or ne'er would the thought, with such thankfulness
    fraught,
Have come, that alone for God's glory he wrought.

So this, suppose I, is the true reason why
In the furrows arust so many plows lie;
From their God-chosen track have the preachers
    turned back
To await the "D. D." they unhappily lack !

When the prophet of old bade Israel behold
The scenes to his view by Jehovah unrolled,
He did not partake of their sins, for the sake
Of "drawing" an audience whenever he spake.

And nowhere can I see, in God's Book of decree,
That for preachers the people a pattern should be;
If 'tis there I've been blind, for I've been inclined
To think the reverse is what Christ designed.

Ah ! surely the Pew must desire that the true,
And not worthless titles, be held up to view !
God's Word in his hand the preacher should stand,
A pure gospel's all that the church doth demand.

Then let preachers be from small vanities free,
If they in the pew would simplicity see ; •
Nor fall in the train of the thoughtless and vain,
Who, thro' titles, to worldy renown would attain.

I have nothing to say of the dress, plain or gay ;
Let the preacher and people adorn as they may ;
'Twas never God's will that the world should stand
    still—
Laws of change and of progress His mandates fulfill.

Love of beauty and art of our life is apart—
To love what is lovely God gave us the heart ;
The gold of the mine, by His wisdom divine,
Was given us to use as our tastes may incline.

With a questioning air there are those who compare
The styles of the present with fashions that were;
And make "much ado" about gems and styles new—
Israel's women had fashions and ornaments too !

And then when I read, with a view to take heed,
Jesus' word—which will truly meet all human need ;
There's never a line about fashion's design,
Or outward adornment, that I can divine.

But clearly to those who would question, He shows,
By purest of logic and plainest of prose,
That all that is sin from a fountain within,
(Not with fashion or unwashen hands) doth begin.

And, if it befall there can be found in all
The church, one too stylish to hear such as Paul,
Deem it not over bold that the church should be told
It were high time to turn such an one from the fold.

On the earth's verdant sod methinks there ne'er trod
A people more true in the worship of God,
Than to-day fill the pews to receive the "glad news"—
O let not the preacher his mission abuse !

But no titles they'll bear in the day heavenly fair,
When from Pulpit and Pew the Redeemed shall meet,
    where,
All radiant with gold and treasures untold,
To their vision the wonders of Heaven shall unfold!

DEATH.

Death, the inexorable, is abroad in our land, gathering recruits for eternity, as the recent departure from our midst of some whose faces had long been familiar, fully attests. Unlike other recruiting officers, he spares neither age, sex nor condition; that he was born, and that he died, commemorating the two important events, alike of the aged and the infant. And the question, "If a man die, shall he live again?" comes to the mind of this generation with the same force that it did to that of the man of Uz, centuries ago; and happy is he who can say with Job: "All the days of my appointed time will I wait till my change come;" adding with full assurance, "For I know that my Redeemer liveth, and that He shall stand at the latter day upon the earth; and though after my skin worms destroy this body, yet in my flesh shall I see God, whom I shall see for myself, and mine eyes shall behold."

It may seem out of place to speak of death here in this sunny land of poetry and song, while the verdure of summer still clothes our woods; and so it would be, if death, like other objects in nature, had its appointed times; but it has not.

> "Leaves have their times to fall,
> And flowers to wither at the north wind's breath,
> And stars to set, but all—
> Thou hast *all* seasons for thine own, O, death!"

Even as I write, only a stone's cast from our door, the remains of one who has sailed out into the unknown seas, are being conveyed to their last resting place; but she leaves behind the sweet assurance that she has fallen asleep to wait a joyful resurrection; and this morning, while mourning friends are missing the feeble voice, and ministering hands are idle and listless, since these ministrations are no more needed, she, in all the brightness and vigor of youth, is singing the song of the Redeemed in Paradise. Longfellow, in his beautiful poetic way, has said:

> "There is no death—what seems so is transition"

But what is death, and what is its office? We

are accustomed to look upon fever as a disease—an
enemy ; but instead hygiene teaches that it comes as
a friend to release us from the grasp of an enemy. So
death comes to open the prison doors of the Christian
—to break the iron bars that intervene, and set the
spirit free.   Then wherefore start at his approach ?

A traveler in foreign countries, weary with
wandering, turns with delight to the home which he
has not seen, it may be, for years.   Hope cheers his
heart, and smiles brighten his face, as imagination
pictures the joy his return will give. But as the fondly-
remembered scenes, familiar haunts, and all the
happy surroundings of home burst upon his sight,
Hope for the first time gives place to Fear—fear that
some loved face was missing; that some shadow has
fallen upon the dear old place.   But this is not the
case with the Christian.   He has constant assurance
that all is well at Home.   His Father is a King, who
permits no evil to come near the dwellers there.   His
Elder Brother is preparing a mansion for him, and
those who enter there will go no more out forever.
Besides, he has more friends and relatives there than
on earth. And he cannot arrive unexpectediy, because
his name is already registered, and "a great multitude
that no man can number," are standing upon the

beach awaiting his arrival; while a convoy of angels has been sent down to escort him over the River. Then, with his passport written upon his forehead, and so many assurances of welcome, why should he doubt and tremble upon the threshold of his Father's House?

LINES.

[Suggested by a sermon preached by Rev. Dr. Hendricks, brother of the late Vice-President of the United States.]

'Twas holy time, and as I sat within
Blest Zion's sacred walls, and heard the words
Of eloquence fall from the stranger's lips,—
The theme, the Passion of our glorious Lord—
My thoughts on wings of Faith were carried back
To Calvary's rugged brow, on which a scene
Transpired, more wildly grand than e'er before
Or since, was witnessed by the sons of man.
'Twas there the blessed Savior of the world,—
The One alone—among the mighty host
That dwell within the Paradise of God—
Found worthy to unclasp the seals that closed
The Book of Life; 'twas there He bled and died,
And 'round its sacred summit cluster all
The hopes, that cheer the heart and buoy it up
Amid the shipwrecks and the storms of life.

How oft by faith the Christian stands
Upon that sacred mountain, and beholds
The mingled stream that gushed from His pierced side;
And almost hears the groans, the dying groans,
Wrung from his anguished soul !

     Nature was shocked
At the unwonted scene—the earth was wrapped
In midnight darkness ; yea, the very sun
Did veil his face, and would not look upon
The awful tragedy ; the rocks were rent,
And earth, sad earth, in wonder, trembled too.
Methinks that loved and loving ones drew near
And looked with anguish on the mournful scene ;—
The mother wept, as only mothers weep ;
And tears, no doubt, in sorrow, gushed from eyes
"Unused to weep !"
  * * * * * *

     But honor to the name
Of Him who reigns alike in Heaven and in
The earth ! The grave refused to hold its dead
And when three days had slowly passed away,
A bright-winged seraph from the upper world
Was sent to roll away the stone that barred
The entrance to the tomb, and Jesus 'rose,

Triumphant Conqueror! and now He stands
Before His Father's throne and pleads our cause.
Consoling thought! that in that city bright—
Whose very streets are paved with purest gold—
Whose pearly gates stand open night and day,
To welcome those who seek eternal rest—
The risen Savior pleads for even me!

Such thoughts as these were passing through my mind,
While listening to the aged man of God,
Whose silvery hair, with wondrous eloquence,
Pointed in silence to the waiting tomb.
I may not look upon his face again,
Nor list' with wrapt attention to his words,
While on the earth ; but in that coming Day,
When cares of life shall be forever past,
When moon and stars shall cease to wax and wane,
And th' heavens are rolled together as a scroll,
And that unnumbered host from East, West, South
And North, which John beheld from Patmos Isle,
Shall gather 'round the judgment seat of Christ,
Methinks I'll see his pleasant face again—
His massive brow encircled by a wreath
Of Amaranthine flowers, and on his head
A crown, bedecked with many brilliant gems.

And then in robes of pure and spotless white—
Washed in the blood that flowed from Calvary—
May we all join the " countless multitude"
To sing the praises of the Lamb throughout
The endless cycles of Eternity !

——

MY GIFT.

I have a gift, sacred and pure,
 And dearer far to me than gold ;
And when great trials I endure,
It is my solace, ever sure,
 And hence its worth cannot be told.

This precious gift, with beauty rife,
 Was given in those tender years,
Ere I had touched the wine of life,
Or known the mock'ry of the strife
 Betwixt its pleasures and its tears.

Mine only !   'Tis a glorious star
 That lights me o'er life-billows wild ;
That sends its radiance afar
To where the dang'rous breakers are,
 And guides me, as I were a child.

Albeit 'tis mine, it is so bright,
  That even strangers, far and near,
Whose pathway leads thro' gloom of night,
And who have suffered from earth's blight,
  Bask in its comfort and its cheer.

And it is sweet as is the breath
  Of asphodel or eglantine,
That upward floats, an incense-wreath,
From censor or from urn beneath,
  When dewdrops sparkle as old wine.

It is a rosy dream of things
  That might have been, that may not be ;
A mem'ry of the past it brings,
And bears upon its shad'wy-wings,
  A vision of futurity.

A star, a breath, a dream, my gift
  Is various—a mixt metaphor ;
Beneath its light, the shadows lift,
Its odor sends ill winds adrift,
  Its dream is gladness evermore.

The fear 'twill be recalled oft clings
  Unto my soul and gives me pain ;
Until I hear the sweep of wings

Fresh from Parnassus' famous springs,
   Then my heart leaps with joy again.

Some tell me 'tis of little worth,
   And class it with inferior things ;
They dream not that it had its birth
In Heaven, not upon the earth,
   And that Heaven's air still to it clings.

To use this gift I'm grown too old,
   Say others, tho' sent from the Throne ;
And yet the Giver hath not told
That e'er a napkin should enfold
   This talent, given for my own;

But that I use it, by His grace,
   For Him—a duty passing sweet ;
Until I, summoned from this place,
To stand before Him, face to face,
   May lay its increase at His feet.

And since the Lord did give it, free,
   I surely feel that it were wrong
To list to those who counsel me
To let it rust or buried be—
   This ever-blessed gift of Song.

DRIFTINGS,

BY MRS. MAY BEDFORD-EAGAN.

"Sleep soft, beloved!" we sometimes say,
Who have no tune to charm away
    Sad dreams that thro' the eyelids creep;
But never doleful dream again
Shall break the happy slumber when
    "He giveth His beloved sleep."

MEMOIR OF MRS. MAY BEDFORD-EAGAN.

In a small cottage, situated on the picturesque banks of the Hondo, in Llano county, Texas, October 23, 1858. May, the eldest-born of John Joseph and Lou Singletary·Bedford first opened her eyes to the pleasures of earth and—its many sorrows. I speak advisedly in this case, and not from any morbid sentimentality, inasmuch as her earliest memories were of the time when civil dissensions were agitating our great country; and when neighbors and friends and kindred were estranged on account of political differences. The scene of one of her first romances, Ruth, was laid in Texas, and the story shows how deeply graven on her heart and memory were the experiences of those troublous times. She was by no means deficient in cheerfulness, but she possessed a degree of thoughtfulness not often observed in one so young, as a result of her surroundings and the fact that the companions of her childhood were mostly those of mature years. In one place she says: "I am so constituted that work and action have seemed pleasure, and I have not had time to think of what was missing. I mean I have not known till now that childhood is past and I have never been a child."

When only four years of age she learned her letters, standing at my side when I was at work, pointing to each letter with her own little fingers. Shortly afterward she started to school, where she soon learned to read. It is fair to state, however, that she was no prodigy; books with her simply took the place of childish companions. As she advanced in years and knowledge, a fine literary taste was manifested in her, which she cultivated more from the personal pleasure to be

derived from it, than from any ambition for the future. She
early formed a habit of committing her thoughts to paper;
and when in college her letters home assumed the form of a
diary, in which she chronicled the occurrences of her daily
life. Before leaving school she contributed several articles to
the press; and when text-books were finally laid aside, she
varied her home duties with literary work. Madeline, Ruth,
Mizpah, Lights and Shadows, and other serials followed each
other so closely one could scarcely realize that literature was
merely the incident and not the main object of her life. But
this was true. When "copy" was called for, she would put
aside whatever was engaging her at the time, and, taking her
pencil, would write, seemingly without any effort of mind—as
if her thoughts were already arranged, as I suppose was the
case; then, often without revising or even glancing over the
manuscript, would send it to the office, and resume her suspended work.

Her reading was extensive and varied. She was especially
fond of Humboldt's Cosmos, geological works, Ruskin's and
others of that class. In accordance with her mood, poet,
philosopher, scientist or novelist became her companion. And
yet so unaffected was she in conversation, and so charming in
manner, that even strangers came under the magnetism of her
gifts and were drawn to her as to a friend. Apropos to this,
a touching incident occurred in connection with a visit which
she made to Mobile in 1882 as correspondent of the Pensacola
Post: While at the Battle House she formed the acquaintance
of a Mrs. Rowe, which seemed mutually agreeable. After
spending a few pleasant days together they separated with little probability of ever meeting again. However, in 1885, Mrs.
Rowe had occasion to stop for awhile in Pensacola, the home
of her sometime friend, and decided to hunt her up. She
called at the postoffice as the most probable place of finding
her address, and made inquiries of the clerks. They could give
her no information, but suggested that she await the arrival

of Mr. Eagan, the postmaster. When he came, she asked if he could tell anything about a young lady whose Christian name was May, and whose father was editor of a Pensacola paper—she had forgotten the surname. The postmaster was so startled he could not speak for some moments. He then replied: "Yes—she was my wife, but she is dead." Mrs. Rowe was greatly shocked and grieved. The incident is given simply as illustrative of the statement that even casual friends did not easily forget her.

As a writer her popularity was phenomenal She depicted life in its true colors, and so touched the great throbbing human heart; and she wrote for the pleasure of writing, as said elsewhere, and not for fame. All through her work there seems to be a looking forward to the beauties of that Unseen Country whose very borderland she was unconsciously treading.

On April 30, 1882, she was married to Mr. John Eagan, a gentleman of great popularity and many personal attractions. Her health had not been good for sometime, and after her marriage she wrote little. She commenced a romance, and had written about one hundred pages when their residence was burned and the manuscript with it. She never attempted to rewrite it. Only one piece written after her marriage has been published, "Breaking Up." It appears at the close of this volume.

Mrs. Eagan professed faith in Christ at eleven years of age, and some years later united with the Baptist church at Columbus, Kentucky, and was baptized in the Mississippi by Rev. C. C. Chaplin. Firm in the faith and doctrines of this church, she was yet tolerant of all other denominations. Her husband had been raised a Catholic, and they had in their home an elegant Catholic family Bible which they sometimes read together She never tried to convince him that the tenets of that people were wrong. Instead, she often went with him to the Catholic church, and then he would go with her to her own. By this means all prejudice was prevented. She once said to me that the one great object of her life was to lead him to become a true Christian. I believe that she succeeded. He promised her on her deathbed that he would meet her in Heaven, though he was not converted until about a year afterward. Since that time his life has been consistent with his profession.

But the life so beautiful and unselfish and full of promise was destined to be short. She came to us at Bay Cottage, our lovely country home which she and I had named on account of the beautiful bay it overlooked and the graceful laurel or bay trees that surrounded it, in the last days of July. Her health had been failing for sometime, and the following day, Tuesday, a physician was called, but we did not apprehend anything serious at the time. On Sunday morning she seemed quite cheerful. In the evening, however, her thoughts took a more serious turn, and she told me she wanted "Shall we gather at the River" sung at her funeral. She then asked me to bring her Mrs. Browning's poems, and from "The Sleep" she selected this stanza to be engraved on her tombstone:

"And friends, dear friends, when it shall be
That this low breath is gone from me,
    And 'round my bier ye come to weep,
Let one—most loving of you all—
Say, 'Not a tear must o'er her fall,
    'He giveth His beloveth sleep'"

She then requested me to sing "How Firm a Foundation;" but for all this I could not think death so near, she seemed so full of hope; and frequently during the succeeding week spoke of what she would do when she got well. But on the next Sabbath—a fitting time for the closing of such a life; we realized that she could not live. When told by her father that she was dying, she lifted her eyes to his and repeated the beautiful words of Job: "I know that my Redeemer

liveth.' I only go before; you will all come." She then gave
directions about her casket and burial robes, requesting that
everything be plain and simple. When done, she turned to
me and said: "I do this that you may not worry over these
things when I am gone." Feeling that the time was short,
she now took an affectionate leave of her weeping friends,
kissing and caressing them tenderly, and expressing regret at
the absence of two brothers. Then, while a sweet smile en-
wreathed her features, lifting her hands upward, without a
struggle, she entered upon that Sabbath of rest that remains
for the people of God—on the 12th of August, 1883, not having quite completed her twenty-fifth year. The funeral at
Milton on the following day was largely attended, the services
being conducted by Rev. J. S. Parks of Pensacola, assisted by
one of the local ministers. A number of the business houses
of the city were closed during the services at the church, a
degree of respect never before paid by that people to one so
young.

Under the heading of "The Death of an Eminent Literary
Lady," a special from Pensacola to the New Orleans Picayune
under date of August 13, says: "The community deeply
sympathize with Mr. John Eagan, collector of internal revenue
for West Florida and a leading member of the city council,
whose wife died at Milton on Sunday afternoon in the very
bloom of a youthful and happy wifehood. Mrs. Eagan, a
daughter of Mrs. Lou Singletary-Bedford, the poetess, was
lovely and accomplished; was possessed of fine literary taste,
and had won recognition as a writer of rare talents. Her amia-
bility had won her troops of friends and admirers. Her untimely death will be profoundly lamented. * * * This afternoon the Odd Fellows lodge, the mayor, and representatives of
the city government, and a large number of citizens took a
special train and attended the funeral at Milton in a body, to
manifest their appreciation of the husband, and their lament
at the demise of his lovely consort."   L. S. B

DRIFTINGS.

Drifting along with the tide, washed hither and yon, these little scraps are thrown into the heaving, surging sea of Literature—it may be to sink to the bottom ; or, rising with the tide, they may be cast upon the shores of some unknown land. They claim no merit in themselves, but are mere fragments which, on the ceaseless waves of Thought, have accumulated, until now they form a heap of scattered ideas, and I have decided to send them out on a frail bark to try what good they may do. If the world likes them many such will be launched to win or lose. What the issue will be who can tell ?

> "Fame's golden temple gleams afar—
> You see the shining gate
> Stand open wide for those who learn
> To work and watch and wait."

Though Fame is not to be desired, success is to be sought ; and if by patient, constant endeavor, it can be attained, and these little papers do any good in the broad field of men, it is all that is expected of them. They are out with the tide :

> " Drifting, drifting to lands unknown,
> From a world of love and care;
> Drifting away to a home untried,
> And hearts that are beating there."

BY AND BY.

There is something so hopeful, and yet so sad, in the little words " By and By." They give a promise of fruition, but at the same time there is a far-off sound of something that is past, and of something you will have to lose now, in order to obtain the prize hereafter. You promise yourself, if your path be dark and dreary, that the joy in the by and by will be greater; that if, with untiring energy, you toil through life, perhaps bruising yourself in the rough places, the rest by and by will be sweeter ; that if pain, sorrow, suffering, poverty, cold, hunger—yes, if all earthly evils afflict you here, that joy, peace, contentment, will be your portion hereafter; that the gentle Christ will be your brother, that his smile will comfort you; and that for the sadness which has been, you will have rest, Heaven, home, by and by.

BROKEN RESOLUTIONS.

I was thinking to-day of the resolutions we are constantly making and breaking. We promise ourselves that we will turn over that oft-turned "new leaf;" that we will lead better, more consistent lives; that we will give up the small (?) sins which we have cherished so long. And we really intend to keep this self-made promise. But the temptation to break it presents itself, and, without considering our resolution, or if we do, it is as something visionary, and consequently not binding, we readily yield. If a friend were to come to us at such a time and say, "You have been guilty of falsehood." we should feel our blood boil, and the fire would flash from our eyes, while in strongest terms we would deny the charge. "But," says the friend, "1 know you are guilty ; you promised YOURSELF that you would quit that habit, and you meant it. God registered that promise. He took note of it, and now—you have broken one of the most sacred vows a person ever made. It was God's Spirit that moved you to make it, and in your hour of weakness you listened to the tempter and—fell."

IMPATIENCE.

Two wee hands were lifted to me, and a baby voice with tears in it, said pleadingly :

"Titi, pease mend me br'aked finger !"

I threw my work aside exclaiming petulantly :

"O Collie! you are such a tease! There is forever something to be done for you! Let me see what is the matter now !"

The little one came forward with her brown eyes filled with tears, and a questioning look on the innocent face. Immediately I regretted my hasty words, and taking the tiny form in my arms, pressed it closely to my heart. The little finger had really been seriously bruised, and needed attention ; but because I did not wish to stop my work just then, I must needs speak crossly to the baby.

That was a great many years ago, and that trusting, guileless child has grown to be a woman. Her pretty wavy hair has become white with trouble and care. Her feet have been pierced by many thorns— her child's heart has been transformed into an aching, troubled woman's heart. Though we were sisters and I many years older than she, I have remained almost young, while she has grown "so old, so weary." My heart is pained when I think how many of her childhood days might have been marked by columns of shining gold; of how many gentle words might have been spoken, instead of the quick, annoying ones which drove deep into the tender heart, and made smarting wounds; and now I repeat over, "patience, patience."

DESPONDENCY.

Sometimes there comes a cloud over the bright sunlit sky of my happiness, and I can see no golden light. Friends seem so far away. I cannot reach them, and they make no effort to come to me. I hear no loving, encouraging words; feel no tender, warm hands upon my brow. My heart beats painfully slow, for just then life is burdensome; I almost wish it were ended, for what is it without love? Then comes another thought. I remember a Garden where a lone Man suffered so that great drops stood on His brow; then another scene where many men scoffed at and reviled Him. No friends came to take Him away, though He was suffering for them—"They all forsook Him and fled." The sky clears. Again I see the sunshine, and O, how beautiful life now appears! I know that my friends have not all forsaken me; and, sweeter still, that my High Priest is watch-

ing and smiling upon me, even though in His agony
His earthly friends "all forsook Him and fled."

> "There is scarcely a line in the Book of books,
>   No matter how often read,
> That saddens me like the little line—
>   'They all forsook Him and fled.'
> In that trying hour when His voice did call,
>   'Why hast Thou forsaken Me?'
> When every sin that held Him in thrall
>   Was a wave of agony;
> When Judas came with his traitor kiss,
>   And others with swords, instead,
> His chosen ones gave a startled look,
>   And 'all forsook Him and fled.'"

WHAT SHALL WE READ?

Sometimes in a fit of desperation, such as the
larger portion of humanity is subject to, we do things
for which our judgment and higher sense of duty
and right afterward reproach us; and in some sense
we are excusable; but when we coolly and deliberately
do wrong, there is no extenuation. no niche through
which we can escape the consequences of our wrong-
doing. There are two kinds of wrong—one, which is
self-evident and needs no explanation; the other is
insinuatingly beautiful, with no scars and marks as a
warning to bright eyes; and often the deepest pitfalls
lie beneath the greenest, longest, and most luxuriant

grass. In all the realm of literature there are few more beautiful writers than Byron and Poe, but beneath the outward garment of beauty there lurks a fearful skeleton. Our libraries are full of works whose musical rhythm pleases the senses, and whose words are the sweetest and choicest our language affords. They clothe sin in a fascinating garb, and hide from us the retribution that must come. They robe sin in its most flowery colors, and every line seems an axiom, every sentence a truth. We read the lines, we take in their beauty, failing to see the sophistry of the arguments. We imbibe the poison, and lose ourselves in a delirious sense of pleasure, but the harm is slowly working its way. We lose all taste for better, purer works. We are blindly seeking after truth, and saying : " Human nature is the best teacher, and these works are the best interpreters of humanity." But it is a mistake. The popular works of the day are not correct pictures of life. They take for their heroes and heroines, weak, pleasure-loving men and women—such as are only now and then found—and make them types of the masses. Impressionable men and women read the works ; they grow to doubt the purity, the genuineness of all actions. They attribute wrong motives to every one, and after awhile life loses all its charm and beauty to them. "There is no truth," they say, and they "have had enough of false."

Burn such books! Throw them away! Cultivate a taste for something better—look at life from a higher standpoint. Search for the good, the true, and doubt all that seems evil. If you want to study human nature, study it from living models, and in every character, no matter how much "besmirched by sin," you will find some good lurking; and so long as one atom of good remains, believe in it. Read purer works than Ouida, Charles Read and others of that class.

UPROOT THE WEEDS.

There is no field in which grass grows but may be cultivated; no weeds which infests the heart but may be uprooted. The roots may be deep, the seed wide-spread, yet time and industry may weaken, and it may be, sometimes destroy them.

MUSIC.

If music does not reach you, if the scent of the rose is dead, let not the thought come that it is not; that it was not. There is not music for us every day, and the flowers fade: but there is hope enough for each hour, and sometimes the music will strike up; some day the air will be full of perfume. Only wait God's time.

THE BETTER WAY.

How much better it is to look into the eastern sky where the sun is, than across the valley where the shadows lie. How much better to see the good in your neighbor and praise it, than to see the evil and speak of it. How much sweeter to believe in truth than in falsehood. If the false seem most, yet know that behind it lies some good; and while in your heart you condemn the evil, seek ever to find the good—be sure it lies somewhere; and if it be possible, draw it out that the world may know and feel it.

THE NEW YEAR.

The New Year! How hopeful and brave are our hearts, how expectant of rich benefits when it shall have grown old. How eagerly we look ahead, and build air castles, all beautiful with rainbow-tinted glass, with enlightened frescoe—how we dream, yet even while we dream the castle begins to fall. Time is rushing on and the rude hand of decay and dissolution grasps ever at the most beautiful part of our castle. We know all this before the shock comes; we

know our castles are but delicate filagree, but then—
they are so beautiful. And even if this year brings
nothing but disappointment and regret, a time will
come after all this waiting, a brighter day will dawn,
when the year will be always new, when the pictures
of the imagination shall be more than realized. Yes,
a new year which shall know no ending, which cannot get old—one long eternity of bliss in a home
where God is ever.

LITTLE THINGS.

If we have realized the meaning of our little acts,
how many of them would take a different coloring!
How many pretty things which, at the time they are
said, mean nothing, would be left unsaid, because of
the sadness they might leave in somebody's heart;
how often we would express love and sympathy instead of mirth and ridicule! Sometimes when we see
even the friends whom we love best placed in un-
pleasant positions the ludicrous side of the picture
strikes us and a gay peal of laughter bursts thought-
lessly from our lips; when, if we could see the bruise
it leaves on somebody's heart we would suppress our
mirth that we might not inflict pain on a friend.
Scarcely a day passes that these little (?) things do
not occur. Sometimes we see our mistakes and could

correct them, but false pride or stubbornness prevents;
friends are estranged and life loses some rays of sunshine for us; some slight pain, some faint regret, lies
hidden away in our hearts; the memory of some
thoughtless word, some heartless laugh, comes like a
shadow and we cannot forget. Sometimes we see a
face we love, with a look of pained surprise in it, and
it follows us for days after; and perhaps the happiness and destiny of a human being hung on one
little act of our lives, and the golden links of friendship have been dissolved by a light word or careless
laugh.

THE NIGHT IS COME.

The pink flush in the western sky spreads itself
over the pines and oaks; the few last leaves which
still cling to the almost bare branches of the trees are
flaming with red; and the faint cry of the boys in
the distance falls dreamily on the ear;

"Bells on the mountain side tinkle and cease,
　Faintly the shadows glide—all is at peace."

The night is come—the day is done; but a faint
red glow stretches across the horizon, and we in-
sensibly think of the morrow; and then a grander
thought comes of that everlasting day which is just
beyond the clouds of earth. Each hour brings us

nearer the dawning. We see the pearl tints in the sky, the golden stars that gem the pure azure, the silvery waters below—all suggestive of a brighter, fairer picture ; and we forget all doubt and skepticism; forget the cold philosophy of Reason, and Faith comes like a benediction ; we KNOW that God is. The student may seek for perfect knowledge in his masterful reasoning, but he ends in doubt. Living faith belongs to the simple, as true love belongs to the brave.

FALLEN LEAVES.

When the yellow light of the October sun falls upon the great forest it burns itself into the leaves, turning them yellow and brown and crimson and gold ; and after a little while they fall to the earth and moulder and decay, or are gathered up by fair hands, pressed and put away—a beautiful memento of one bright season. The days go on, the leaves lie hidden away until some day, when the rain is falling drearily on the roof and windowpanes, when the time hangs heavily, the leaves are brought out from their hiding place and grouped and arranged into a wreath or bouquet. They recall the past; they bring thoughts of another autumn season that is "to be," and the links of the Before and After stretch themselves over

a vast Eternity—all because of these little fallen
leaves. Life is so full of such little and seemingly
trifling incidents; and yet these little things preach
great sermons; these dainty nothings are powerful
reminders. Rough little pebbles sometimes prove to
be rare jewels. Do not despise leaves and pebbles;
you know not what lessons they may teach. You
know not the ways and means of their creation, nor
why God gave them form. And if the leaves are
spotted and decayed, remember that even in that
God's hand is to be found.

THE BUNCH OF LILACS.

Once a little child gave me a bunch of lilacs.
The pretty delicate blossoms were crushed by childish
hands, the stems were broken, and the flowers drooped
helplessly, but the sweet voice said in lisping tones:

"Pitty f'owers for 'ou; me brin' 'em to 'ou to put
in 'o' hair."

I stooped and took the flowers; then raising the
little one in my arms I kissed the baby lips and
hugged the childish form. And though four long
years have passed since I saw the little one, and the
flowers lie shattered from their stems in an old school
book which is seldom opened now, I can never forget

that the child who gave them, came to me when I was
tired and homesick—was far away from home and
friends; and the simple gift, the babyish words, were
more to me than the stinted sympathy and polite
friendship of older persons could have been. I can
never forget how like the sound of sweet music the
child's voice fell on my ear. And though I had never
seen the child before, and have never seen it since, I
love it. And when many greater events of my life
shall have been forgotten, the memory of that sweet
face and baby voice, and the bunch of lilacs, will remain as a pleasant perfume after the flowers are
faded.

REST.

How we speak this little word—what music is
condensed within this one syllable—REST. What
bright dreams of happiness dance before our tired
eyes, as we think of the rest awaiting us when we
shall have accomplished our task. No rest can come
without labor, for, without exertion, we feel no need
of it. We spend the day in physical labor, and in
the evening comes rest—for the body; but for the
mind no perfect rest is to be attained. The mighty
machinery of our brain is constantly at work—the

wheel of thought never ceases its grinding. Long
years of existence pass away ; childhood merges into
youth, youth into manhood, manhood into age, and
age almost forgets to count them, as they glide rapidly
by, and still the brain has NEVER rested. There would
be no need of rest for the mind if the thoughts
evolved were always happy scintillations; but the
clouds more frequently dim the horizon of Reality,
and it is only when wandering through the pictured
halls of Imagination that we can see the sun in all
its glory lighting up the beautiful scenery created by
Fancy's fairy frostwork. But all too soon grim Reality
seizes upon the mind, the sunlight vanishes, and
again we have new difficulties to contend with; but,
through it all, we have the promise of a rest beyond,
to cheer and comfort us. We are to work here, for
God's glory; and we know that when the clouds are
darkest, when the waves beat most relentlessly, we
have a "Rock that is higher than we" under whose
shadow we can find rest—sweet rest.

A loving arm is always extended to us, and a
gentle voice says, "Come unto Me, all ye that labor,
and are heavy laden, and I will give you rest;" and
again, "Learn of Me, for I am meek and lowly in
heart, and ye shall find rest unto your souls." How

considerate, how thoughtful, in the Master, thus to propose to bear our burdens, to lighten our cares, and when we are tired, to give us rest!

Then let us "work for Him while it is day, for the night cometh when no man can work;" a time when the tired hands will be folded across the lifeless, soulless bosom of the clay; when the hair will be smoothed back from the temples that have ceased to throb with pain, and all will be at peace. What a blessed hope we have of rest in that bright home, where there is "no need of the sun, neither of the moon, to shine in it; for the glory of the Lord doth lighten it." And in those glorious mansions which Jesus has gone to prepare, there is room for all; and when "the silver chord shall be loosed, or the golden bowl be broken, or the pitcher be broken at the fountain, or the wheel be broken at the cistern,"—then comes the reward—a Crown of Life, studded with stars; a robe of Immortality; a Home with the Father; a meeting with loved ones who have gone before; and finally, rest,—sweet, eternal REST.

LITTLE INCIDENTS.

It is certainly true that little incidents, to which we attach no consequence, are often the hinges upon which hang the most important events. A word, an act, an impulse, may exert an influence over our whole future; may reach down through the dim labyrinths of Time, up through the golden gates of Eternity, to the judgment bar, even to the heavenly jury. We go on doing whatsoever our hands find to do, little dreaming that we are spellbound by a thoughtless act of childhood.

TREAD OF YEARS.

When we are happy the years seem to fly; but when sorrow and care weigh us down, and we are of the earth, earthy, each day has a meaning of too deep import to be forgotten, and leaves a scar to remind us that we have suffered. When scar after scar defaces the landscape of years; when our sky is overcast with clouds instead of light; then time is leaden-paced. Youth always measures time by itself—counts forward, and not backward. Add to the years of childhood, darkness and gloom, and imagine the interminable waste of a future with nothing to hope for —the life stretching before the child.

ASHES OF ROSES.

I sit here on the river banks watching the clouds as they float far away in the distance, or forming themselves into strange shapes, are reflected in the clear waters at my feet. Far off yonder looms a great stone boulder, grim, and grey, and cold. Beyond it rises a mountain chain that seems enveloped in a blue mist, such as we have often seen real mountains wear. Here and there, light, feathery clouds are floating, growing more rugged, more grand. But silently a change is being wrought. A red flush appears at the edges of the clouds, then spreads farther and grows deeper until the whole sky seems in a flame. Then slowly

> "Bright daylight closes,
> Leaving where light doth die
> Pale hues that mingling lie—
> Ashes of roses."

The pearl and pink tints blend and grow into one broad, rippling, wave-like sea of beauty. The day is done, and what remains? Ashes of roses. Yes, the brightness, the glory of the day is past, but behind the stars another day is heaving into birth, which will perhaps end as this one has done, leaving—ashes of roses.

Every hope, every ambition, every dream of our life, falls short of its promise, and all along our pathway are scattered—ashes of roses. We build our hopes too high for attainment color our dreams all too bright for reality, allow our thoughts to grasp too much for our weak hold, and the result is—ashes of roses. And so it is better as it is; better that we find our strength is not infinite; better to learn that God is God, and therefore Strength and Wisdom and Power, that we may feel our dependence upon Him;

> "When love's warm sun is set
> Love's brightness closes;
> Eyes with hot tears are wet,
> In hearts there lingers yet—
> Ashes of roses."

But when we have learned all this; when we have held the flower in our hands, and have seen it wither and fade; when sadly the brightness, the hopefulness of youth fades out, leaving in our hearts only the memory of what was—only the ashes of life's roses; then comes the reality of something which cannot decay; which cannot turn to ashes, but will always be fair and glorious. Then comes God's love and care; a day which holds no dead hopes, no broken dreams; a day all lovely and beautiful, when we can close our eyes, fold our hands, and pass away to that better home where we will be no more mocked with the—ashes of roses.

GOD'S ACRE.

Saturday evening a soft mist lay over land and sea, and the balm of earth's beauty touched my country-bred heart. I could not stay in doors, so putting on a hat and arming myself with a sketch book, I went off for a ramble, seeking the spot freest from noise and bustle; for the stillness of a summer's day filled the air, and the calm of romantic speculation was in my brain. For a time I walked on, with no special point in view—simply dreaming; but after awhile I found myself in "Potter's Field." Quiet? Yes, perfect quiet here. The old oaks that reach up to heaven, were mute. All around lay ranks and files of the dead. In the farthest corner of the "field," are the graves of past and forgotten generations— men and women who trod for a brief hour the stage of life—men and women whose names, as their bodies, are passed away and forgotten. These graves are walled up by an arched brick or cement covering, but no name, no date. Dead!—lost to earth and its interests, with nothing to tell whether they were men, women or children passed away. It is pitiful. The children who perhaps owe their existence to these people of a younger time in Pensacola's existence, are left in ignorance of where they rest. Grass and briers grow in tangled luxuriance here—weeds and brush hold high carnival over the bodies of God's children. Dead! Forgotten! Let the weeds grow—the briers spread—they are not of us.

Heavens! how sad it is that they should be so neglected. There are tender little children lying here —babes who were loved and caressed on earth, now covered over with tangled masses of weeds and briers; men and women accustomed to the luxuries of earth sleeping neglected and forgotten. Can it be that men know this—do they think so lightly of the dead? Mothers, fathers, friends gone away, and no loving hand left near to keep clean the graves of their dead. Why does not our city employ a sexton to watch over God's Acre, and preserve from neglect the sleeping dust of her people—to do the work which friends may not do? Here and there one comes upon a pretty clean lot where loving hearts still beat for the silent sleepers ; but there are hundreds who have fallen asleep, strangers in a strange land, and the briers are choking them. Is this Christian-like? Is there no help for it? The burial place of Pensacola, one of the oldest in the United States, is a link between the centuries that are gone and the present. The people who have gone and those who yet live are as one, and we owe the Past a measure of respect. Let us make of this neglected field a God's Acre, truly ;—consecrated, calm, peaceful—such as shall not be a reproach to us.

CATCHING THE SUNSHINE.

"What are you doing my little one ?" asked a young mother of her innocent baby of seven summers.

"Catching the sunshine, mamma. See how it hides. When I step in here to get it, it is gone, and I go away and then it comes back, and I do wish I could hold it—everything looks so pretty in the sunshine. You know those zenias that grow in the garden ? Well, yesterday night I looked at them and they were old and faded; but this morning I went to see them and they were real pretty. Don't you guess they have been catching the sunshine is the reason ? And yesterday papa said my hair looked like threads of gold when the sun shined on it—I reckon it was catching the sunshine too. Everything looks pretty when the sun shines on it."

The little one went back to her play, quite unconscious of the impression her childish words had made. The mother leaned her head on her hand, and looked out on the beautiful earth. Everything was bathed in a flood of golden light, but away over the hills, a little cloud, "not bigger than a man's hand," sailed alone. There was a far-away look of sadness in her eyes, as she thought of her little one who had scarcely counted her "seven times one," and to whom life seemed but a long path of happiness and sunshine. She thought of the years to come, of the trials in store for her darling, and her heart was sad, and in her sadness, she forgot to catch the sunshine of the present and let the future take care of itself..

*   *   *   *   *   *

Again the mother sat in the same room. The years had dealt heavily with her—the loved form of him whose arm had been her stay through life was missing. He had gone to the land where "the sunshine ever lingers," and her baby alone remained with her—a baby no longer, but a lovely young girl whose years numbered little more than "seven times two." She stood beside her bereaved parent, and tried to point out the roses that yet bloomed for her along life's rugged steeps. She saw the sunshine still decking "hill and vale, and stream," and would not repine, but as in her infant days continued to "catch the sunshine."

Years rolled on—for the cycles of time will not stop, and changes are ever going on around us—and we see no longer the innocent child, or fair young maiden, but instead, a woman advanced in years. Have the years made her bitter and misanthropic? Let us see.

Her girlhood days passed happily, womanhood came, and long ago she gave her heart into the kindly care of her choice. Little faces sprang up around her, sunny heads nestled on her loving breast, childish voices called her by the sweet name of "Mother," and she loved them better than her own life. She pointed them to the Father's Home, told them of the angels clothed in beauty, of the Shepherd's tender care for the little ones, and they loved the heavenly home more than the earthly one, and they unfolded their little wings and went up higher, where they would ever retain the sunshine. For a time the mother's heart rebelled; but at length she loved to think of her darlings as her angels, and she counted the links in the golden chain that was stretched down from Heaven to draw her upward. After awhile the last link was added, and her noble and loving husband stepped beyond, to await with his children for the coming of the wife and mother.

Did she grow discouraged? No. Her belief in the Father's wisdom was unshaken, her faith simple and childlike; and by her deeds she was adding jewels to the crown that was awaiting her in the Hereafter. By and by, after a long day spent on earth, catching the sunshine of God's love, she gently folded her hands over her peaceful breast, and said, while a heavenly smile lit up her face, "Mother, Husband, Children, I too am coming up there to 'catch the sunshine.'"

LIFE'S MISERERE.

Sometimes, we scarcely know why, the days are sorrowful, dreamy, and full of vague forebodings. Even the sunlight seems less joyous, there are promises of rain in the air, and every sound that floats across the other bears a melancholy tone. O how wearisome! We go out on the highways, away into the woods,—deep into Nature's heart; but the wind's whisper among the leaves, and the wild bird-notes, float out on the air with the same mournful cadence.

The little stream glides along noiselessly for a time, then rushes impetuously along the banks, over roots and rocks, as if to get beyond its sluggish bed—this still despair. We look up into the foilage above, and vague, restless shadows seem flitting there—shadows of things beyond our ken ; we look through the pines into the distance, and the shadows multiply. The crows flying overhead sing sadly, despairingly ; the bell's tinkle in the distance sounds like a refrain from sad music ; the woodman's axe echoes dreamily along the river side. We look over the glittering stream of waters, and again we see the "shadow of some pain." We look up at the sky, and the dreamy azure, dotted here and there with deeper blue and snowy white, seems to concentrate the full sadness of nature in itself ; and we throw ourselves on the ground and give vent to our feelings.

The days of childhood appear to our vision, and we see the old schoolhouse, and the great poplars and sycamores, beneath which we played such rare games of "base" and "wolf over the snow ;" we hear the familiar voices of our schoolmates calling out clearly, remember our childish friendships and quarrels, nor do we forget the hard lessons in multiplication and division, and the terrible puzzles in parsing ; but notwithstanding these blemishes in the restrospect, we feel what happy, happy days they were, and would that we could live them over.

Then we recall the time when we were "big," and bade farewell to the old log schoolhouse and went away to college. O those, too, were happy days— days of high hopes, of brave wishes and great ambitions—days when all the world was ours, and we had but to say, "I will." Yes, those were happy days! I see the old college now, as it stands on the hill with its miles and miles of beautiful trees, its hills and valleys lying around it ; see the grand old maple, the monarch of all the trees in the grounds ; yes, see it in its September glory, with its gorgeous color of yellow, and crimson, and brown, and pupils scattered here and there in groups; hear the sound of the croquet balls and mallets, and above all, I see the dear old principal standing on the upper step of the portico looking at "his children." Thus we recall the scenes of our youth and live in them again, but in spite of us the retrospect is sad. The thought that the golden hours have fled, and left no mark ; the thought that it has been in our power to live nobler lives than we have done, comes to us with a strange rebuke, for we are conscious of having wasted one part of life's grand possibilities. And yet, these vain regrets, these long-ings after the hopelessly lost, lend a charm and a value to the past. The joys of the past increase, the sorrows decrease, by retrospection. We ever stand on the shores of Uncertainty, yet have faith in the ships which Time will wreck all along the sea of life.

The lives we lead are full of sadness, but all sad-ness has a refrain of hope—all sorrow is followed by joy. Thank God that He sometimes sends us sorrow, for by it we measure our blessings. It is one of His agents. There is no life but has had days of dark-ness, no day but has been overshadowed by some faint regret; but in these shadows, if we look, we may see God. Where the shadows are, there God is, and into all hearts he can send the sweet perfume of love and peace.

I once knew a woman whose whole life was a shadow. Just in the dawn of womanhood, when life, to most of us, is illumined by bright hopes and sweeter dreams, she, the fairest bud in "a rose-bud garden of girls," was stricken with a night of years— a night into which no hope of daylight could come. Many times I met this beautiful saint, and though she could not see me, I felt that her pure soul could read my very thoughts. Did she ever complain? Did she

waste her time in lamenting her blindness—in pining
for the sight of beautiful things? Never. Her lips
dropped pearls—her life was a living sermon ; and if
ever a complaint passed her lips, only God and the
angels heard it. Many times I have heard her say,
as if to encourage others, and all unmindful that she
was sorest afflicted :

> " What tho' the road be rugged,
>   And the sky be seldom bright,
> Since every footstep leads us
>   To the lovely Land of Light."

When we compare our own sorrows with the
trials and sufferings of others, it seems so weak and
selfish to complain, or even let sad feelings creep into
our hearts for there are many sunbeams, and they
yield.infinitely better than clouds. Then

> " Back, back, O tears! We have no cause to mourn—
> Sighs break in songs upon the other shore,
> And grief is lost in gladness evermore."

MAUD ARNOLD.

CHAPTER I.

I cannot tell how I found out all these items in my heroine's life. Life is too short for long explanation, but what I write is true. Maud Arnold is as real a character as I am—as I who write these things. I have known her since her childhood; we have grown up together. We have had our quarrels and our makings up, as others have since the world began. To me she has ever been the embodiment of all that is lovable. Faulty and fallible as she is, she is yet a heroine. I have a little red morrocco book in my keeping, in which she tells her childish troubles, and describes, with her own honest simplicity, her little voyage over the sea of childhood. She may tell you all this, for I know I can never equal her; and you may learn from her something of our first meeting— of our growth in mind and heart. You may read these pages, and you will hold them sacred—as I do ; you will see how troublous was the dawn, and understand how she became a woman even before she was a child.

   *   *   *   *   *

SEPTEMBER 15, 18–.—Well, I am Maud, and that isn't saying much, either, for I haven't anything to boast of in saying it. My father is my hero, and I am going to tell you about him. I think you will like him—I do. I guess you have read John Halifax. Well, father is a grander, nobler man than he, and that is saying a great deal, for John Halifax is one of my ideals of manliness. Ages ago my father was a rich man. My grandfather was an English noble-man's youngest son; he came to the New World to find the justice and wealth denied him in the Old. When he reached here—a young lawyer struggling for the position for which his education and acquirements fitted him; he had no friends, no wealth—nothing but his own strong will and high aims. But fortune favored him. He made friends—and money, too. After awhile he married a true. sweet woman, who loved him for himself. I never knew my grandfather —he died when I was a little cross baby in long dresses; but I knew my grandmother, and I do not wonder that my father is the noblest man in the world, his mother was so good, so grand.

When my father was sixteen, he had to leave college on account of ill health—that is why he never completed his education. This was hard to bear, for he was ambitious. and wanted to become a great law-yer like grandfather, but fate was against him, and he had to give up. But he was a Christian; and he went on doing the duties he had strength to do. No;

I guess I am giving you a somewhat wrong idea of
father's goodness, for perhaps you will imagine that
he was a quiet, patient man, who did good because it
was natural. I reckon that is a beautiful kind of
goodness ; but father's goodness is better. He is a
quick, impulsive, ardent man, and has many temptations, many difficulties to combat against. I know
this, for I am like him in disposition, though not in
character. I have all these trials and temptations ;
and father talks to me about them and shows me the
best ways to act ; though I don't half the time take
his advice ; for I am headstrong. I like to do my
own way—so does father; but he is generous, and con-
siders other people's comfort and happiness. I con-
sult my own pleasure. Father is a Christian, I am a
heathen. I keep a picture of ugly old Budda in my
room all the time, though of course I don't worship it
—I am not superstitious enough for that ; but I like
to imagine him as the heathens did ; I like to think
of the heathen worship anyway. No ! I am not a bit
of a Christian, and I never read my Bible. I read
the Koran, though,—and the Talmud. But I do that
because all smart people do—and I am going to be
very smart when I grow up. I am right smart now !
I have read a great deal of history. I have read
Humboldt's Cosmos, in German, Schiller and Goethe.
I like the languages, and learn them very fast. My
mother is the daugther of a German Professor, and I
have known German since I was a little thing. I

have a good knowledge of French, too. You see I am somewhat of a book-worm—I am only eleven now, and I am always going to study hard. I do not know many people—have never been from home much yet. And I have no one to talk to when father is away, for my mother has so many other children that she hasn't much time to talk to me; and then I believe she loves her boys best anyway. I am the oldest, and have four, no, five brothers. But father loves me, and O, how I love him! I wish you knew father. When I grow up and become a great writer, I am going to write a history of his life. I know you would like him if you knew him—everybody does

Before I was born my father had lost all his property and was a poor man. I was born in St. Louis when he was on his way to California, where he was going to see if he couldn't get rich again. We were awful poor in those days. I have heard mother say we were as poor as church mice. We lived in a little hut down by the river, and didn't even have enough to eat. St. Louis wasn't as large eleven years ago as it is now—you know it isn't an old city. My father caught fish for us when we had nothing else to eat—though I don't guess I ate much, for I was only two months old when we left there. My father had quarreled with his brother who was older than himself and was his guardian. He was always a determined kind of man, and wouldn't do as his brother wished; but went off and married. That made my

uncle mad, and he wouldn't help father any. As
father was under age, he couldn't do anything with
his property. I don't understand how it was; but I
know that when my father was of age, the property
had been so managed that he couldn't get anything.
I don't think there was anything to get, for it had all
been "sunk"—I think that's what they called it.
Well, when father found that he had been defrauded,
he just did the best he could for his two sisters, and
then went away from Kentcky. When he got to St.
Louis, he had no money. He could find work enough,
for the city was growing, but he was always a delicate
man, and he couldn't do much without its almost
killing him. And the worst of all, I was a baby.
Now if I had been big enough, I could have made
money enough for us, but I was not big, you see,—
and that's the reason we had all that trouble! I think
there is where the mistake was made—don't you?
Father says he has made a great many mistakes;
but everybody has—I know I have. I have heard tell
about all this so much, that I sometimes think may
be I remember it. One day father went all over the
city trying to find something to do; and now it was
growing dark, and he had found nothing. He was
standing on the river bank away from the noise of the
city; and was wondering if it would be very wicked,
if he should drown himself. He was thinking that
he was no use to mother and me; and if he were
dead, she would go back to her father, and support

herself by teaching music. So he sat down and wrote her a note telling her all about it and asking her forgiveness. (I have read it myself, for mother has always kept it.) Then he kneeled down and prayed to God to take care of us. When he arose he didn't feel like he wished to die; and stepping back a little, his foot struck against something hard, and stooping down, he picked it up and found it to be a five dollar gold piece. He returned to the busy city; and when he came home, he brought some of the comforts of life.

It seems strange to me even now, for I have never seen any nice people who were as poor as we were. All the poor people I have ever known, were rough, uneducated people; but father says there are a great many refined people whom adversity has brought as low as we were. I know that my father is not rough, lazy or ignorant, (and I guess other people must be the same way,) and his misfortunes have been unavoidable.

I believe I was going to tell about our going to California—wasn't I? Well, after father found the money, he became more hopeful, and went to work with renewed earnestness to find such employment as his strength would permit him to do. He says he thinks God sent him help and friends at this time; for the next day he met a man who had large mining interests in California which he could not go out to attend to himself; and seeming to take a fancy to

father, employed him. In a little while we were in
California. As he wished mother and me to be with
him, he took us to the mining district.

The first that I remember at all in my short life
is about the miners, and how they loved me and
would beg mamma to let me come to their camps;
and I think it was so nice there—for they always did
whatever I wanted them to! Mamma was so kind to
them that they loved her like the poor people loved
Romola.

Father used to say that I was better than a
missionary to them, for they never drank or used bad
language when I was about. I used to go to the
camps every day. When I was six years old I used
sometimes to run off from mamma and go there, for
she had two other babies then, and I didn't like to
rock the cradle and play with them all the time. But
whenever I did this some of "my boys,"—as they
taught me to call them, when I first learned to talk—
would take me in their arms and carry me home; for,
much as they loved me, they wouldn't let me stay
with them without my mother's consent, and they
would always ask if "she" said so. When I learned to
read I used to go and read the Bible to them of eve-
nings; and they would sit in a circle around me with
their hats off listening to the words of life; and when
it was time for me to go, two of them would take me
home. I think it was nicer there than anywhere else
in the world, and I wish we could have stayed there

always; but father's business called him to the city, and we came with him. Some of "my boys" cried when I came away, and I cried too. I was eight years old then, but I didn't know any one except the miners and my parents. I know others now, for it has been three years, and I am better satisfied; still, I would like to go back, for "my boys" loved me, and the people here do not; and I would rather be loved than anything else in the world—I think it makes people the happiest. When I am grown up I intend to go where everybody will love me—I mean to be smart too! And I guess may be I'd better quit being a heathen, for they might not love me if I'm a heathen; so I'm going to commence reading my Bible again. I guess I can be smart and read my Bible too—father reads his, and he is smart.

SEPTEMBER 18.—This is not a book for anybody to read but myself. The way I came to think of writing it, is this: I saw an old woman once who said she had outlived "the memory of her youth"— and it made me feel sad to think of one's forgetting the past; and I thought that may be I might live a long time and might forget; and so I am going to write it all down, and when I am old I can read it, and then—may be sometimes I'll have children of my own who will want to read it.

I started to school yesterday, and as I had never been before, it all seemed so strange. There were a great many girls there—more than I ever saw to-

gether before. I've never seen many girls, for since
we came here mamma has not let me go out; and it
made me feel strange when I went into that great
room—the girls stared at me so. I know if I had
been in their places I should have not done so. Most
of them were dressed finer than I, but I didn't think
that made any difference before. Mamma is as kind
and polite to persons who dress plainly as to those
who dress ever so nicely. It made me feel ashamed
for those girls to see that they noticed my cotton dress
and thick shoes. It made me feel like I never wanted
to know anybody but "my boys." It made me angry
that a girl should do so. I thought all girls were good
and sweet—I thought they would all be better than I.
O, it made me sorry, so sorry—I wish I was back
at the old camps—O, I wish I was there where they
love me!

SEPTEMBER 20.—I have been at school three days
now; and in my studies, I am ahead of every girl of
my age in school—away ahead of them, and I am so
glad! The teachers are all good, and I love them;
and some of the girls I like very much now, but none
do I love so dearly as I used to think I should. But
I don't care so much now as I am not so much of a
stranger, and they are all kinder than I at first
thought—perhaps it was my own fault that they
seemed hateful. Every girl in school has a special
friend but me. It isn't that they are not so good as I
am—some are a great deal better; but I don't love

them very dearly—I wonder why ? May be I am hateful in my ways—anyway, I am not like them; I wish I was, or, at least, a little more like them than I am. I think it would be so nice to have a girl friend of my own, my very own—who could look up into the sky as I do, and feel in sympathy with my thoughts. I don't think I am smart enough yet to have very wise thoughts, but I feel sometimes as if I would fly to pieces if I couldn't find some one who would listen to me. I guess the other girls feel that way too, but they have some one to talk to—some one who is not too "grown up"—some one who doesn't look up with such surprise and wonder at them when they say. things. Papa understands me, but he is too "grown up;" and so there is no one for me to talk to and love as the other girls do—it's too sad, too sad !

FEBRUARY 10.—It has been a long time since I wrote anything here—almost five months. I have been advanced in my classes and am getting along ever so well. But the best of all is this : one day about two months ago, a new pupil came to school—a girl different from any one I ever saw. She is not pretty—not even as pretty as I am ! The girls all commented on her when she came, and I know what they think. They say she is ugly, and it may be true; but I think her prettier than anybody I ever saw, but it is not outside beauty ; it is deep down where but few see it—I see it. She understands me and I love her, and now I am happy. She lives close

to us—her name is Katharine Carlile. She is four
years older than I, but I feel like we were the same
age. We study and read and talk—O, how we do talk!
She is a Christian and tells me how she feels, and it
only shows me how wicked I am ; I am disobedient to
mamma, and unkind to my brothers—am naturally
hateful. Kathie is not quite as well advanced in her
studies as I, but she is a great deal smarter in other
things. She sings beautifully—it seems to me that
the angels do not make sweeter music. If her father
is ever able, he will send her to Italy to have her
voice cultivated. Mr. Carlile has only two children.
His son, Paul, is away, and I have not seen him.
Kathie has his picture, taken ten years ago. I don't
think it pretty, but she says he is beautiful now ! and
O, so smart! I'll be sorry when he comes home, for
then I'll have to give up Kathie—she will not be all
my very own any longer. Now this is wicked of me.
Kathie wouldn't say such things ; she is always
generous; but oh, I can't give her up to Paul; but
then he will not be home for four years, and I needn't
begin to feel bad about it yet !

Kathie and I study very hard. I am going to be
a teacher. I would like to write books ; I love to write
better than anything else in the world, but I must do
something to make a living, and I can't ever write
well enough to make it in that way. Nobody but
Kathie knows that I ever write anything—I wouldn't
let any one else know; and she asks me for every

piece of paper I scribble on. But she is a genius—
she writes beautifully, sings divinely, paints ex-
quisitely—does everything well. In her presence I
feel as if I were in a different world. Mamma says
her society is ennobling and elevating.

CHAPTER II.

OCTOBER 18.—To-day I am fifteen years old—
fifteen, a woman. O, how strange it seems that I am
almost grown up. I am glad, though, for there is so
much for me to do in the world—so much that I
ought to do. Papa is breaking down, and mamma is
getting every day more dependent on me. I have to
plan and think, and think and plan each day, for
something to cheer papa up. It almost breaks my
heart to see him so worn and weary ; so tired of
everything. I think he cannot live long, and if he
should die, then, God help me !

OCTOBER 20.—Such a beautiful thing has happened to-day ! God sent me a gift—one I have prayed
for all my life; a beautiful little sister—a perfect
little angel who came down, I verily believe, on wings
and dropped them at the door, and the other angels
have carried them back to keep for her. It does not
seem true that I should really have a sister—a beautiful little baby sister ! And O, I love her so ! And I
am to be her god-mamma—think of it ! O you dear,
dumb old book, why can't you laugh with me—I am
so glad ?

OCTOBER 22.—Mamma may die, they say—it is terrible! Mamma dead! I can't think of it! And then I have been wicked and hateful to her all my life. If she dies I will feel like a murderer, for I have many, many times been angry and hateful to her. O God! spare her and I will be better to her!

OCTOBER 28.—She is better—she will live; and I am almost wild, I am so happy! But she can't sit up for ever so short a time, and I am to be baby's nurse —I am to wash and dress the dear beautiful little angel every day, and I do so love it! You should only see her beautiful eyes—so big, so brown, so soft —they seem so full of wonder at everything; I think she is comparing this home with the one she left in Heaven. She is as good as can be, and never cries much; and when I put her in the bath, she is too beautiful for anything! I believe I'd kiss her to death if they'd let me! Kathie comes over every morning to see her take her bath. She says baby is the sweetest and most beautiful creature on earth. She and I are even now—she has Paul and I have baby. Everybody wants to name her Paula; and for Kathie's sake I am willing. Mr. Paul is at home now—came while mamma was so ill. I haven't seen him yet, but he is coming with Kathie this evening. I hope I will like him. Baby is asleep now and I think I will run out in the woods a little while. I am so tired and perhaps my head won't ache. * * * It is evening now and Kathie and her brother have been here.

Mr. Paul is a handsome man, I think; but he is
awfully "grown up" and wise, and—I don't like him.
He is going away to-morrow night. I think he ought
to love Kathie very much, for she loves him better
than anybody; but I don't believe he does, and if I
knew he didn't I'd hate him,—everybody ought to
love her, she is so sweet, so good. I don't believe he
loves anybody—he looks so cold and proud ; but he
smiled beautifully at baby, and maybe he is kind.

OCTOBER 18.—October again, the month of my
hardest trials and greatest sufferings—the month of
ill omen to me. Sorrow, grief, despair seem to
crown this one month. There is a melancholy cadence
in every sound—a sombre tint in every ripening leaf.
Two years have come and gone since I wrote a line
here, two busy years rounded up and running over
with work. I have had no time to think of this companion of my childish solitude. But to-night a vague
unrest—an unutterable sense of sorrow—hangs over
me, and I seek comfort here. My little darling is
sleeping. The fierce fever seems to have spent itself,
and she is resting at last. Dear little Paula, sweet
comforter, how I have loved you ! How angry I have
been with God for striking you with the terrible fever!
But you will live now, my sweet, beautiful, brown-
eyed darling ! O how I love the child ! How I dream
and plan for her future. She will be a lovely woman
—lovelier than any one I know ; and if God spares
me I will try to make it bright for her. O, Paula, my

life would have been so dead without you! My two-year old darling, how sad, how desolate it has been with you lying here so sick! I didn't know any one could grow so fond of a little thing like her, but she seems dearer to me than my own life. I love my father—God only knows how well; I love mamma and the boys and Kathie; but Paula came in answer to a prayer. She is a gift of God to me, and I have claimed her as my own these two years. I have never been parted from her a day—never let any one else care for her, and my wild eager heart clings to her—my beautiful, beautiful Paula!

OCTOBER 21.—Did God ever give a good gift and then curse it? O! silence! O, grand, impenetrable Darkness, answer me! Is God a Father who loves His children? Can He love and curse them? Would God, the Father, the Creator, do as revengeful man does? Then is God less than man—then is God tyranical, unjust? Let me curse Him and die.

OCTOBER 28.—My heart is broken, my faith is spent. From now on the world is blank, blank—void of goodness and mercy. The world seems all too desolate for my darling. O, my darling, readily would I with my seventeen years of knowledge of good and evil have taken this burden of years—this sorrow of life from you; but it may not, cannot be. I feel I am too great a coward for this—too great a coward to bear this burden through all the sad, sad years. How can I meet it—this sorrow that God has sent? Is there a God? Then how could He strike my heart as He has done? How crush out my hopes, my dreams, my ambitions, and blast my darling's life, if he is God? No! It cannot be that God has done this thing.

OCTOBER 31.—I have had many comforters and sympathizers, but how can they know anything about it? They do not know—it is I that love her—our darling; and she is—blind—.

Speak low; tread softly; let no harsh word disturb the sorrowful ones. Let not idle curiosity look upon the sacredness of their grief. You may never have known sorrow, and you can not feel with them. Only God can understand the depth and nature of our grief. He it was who laid the chastening rod across our hearts. He it was who gave and then deprived— He blessed, but we heeded not the richness and beauty of that blessing; and in an hour when .we thought not, the light, the glory, the beauty faded, and left us with sore hearts. How we had loved those beautiful brown eyes, so full of innocent joy! The stars never seemed more beautiful than they. So full of love, she seemed formed for happiness. We built many a fairy castle for her. The pretty baby hands that smoothed our brow so tenderly seemed all too fair and soft to come in contact with a rough world. We planned and worked, worked and planned, for her future. We would have had her path flower-strewn and fragrant. She was our baby—our almost idol.

Yes, there the fault lies—we loved the creature more than the Creator—the casket more than the jewel. We built our hopes on mortality.

Our picture was painted after the models of man. We wanted to give our baby all the blessings of earth, and forgot the Creator of that baby—forgot her hereafter. There lay our sin. Inasmuch as we idolized the image, the Father became the immortal Iconoclast to break that image in its most beautiful part, and left us what? Health, life, youth, purity—all this He left us; but He took from her innocent face its light. He left—O, how it hurts me to write it!—our darling blind! Only two short years was she permitted to see the faces she loved. Only two summers did she see the earth in its loveliness. Henceforth her brown eyes are dim, sightless, sealed. The birds may sing, the waters dance and ripple; the faces that her baby eyes loved to look on may light up with smiles, or grow dim with tears; the seasons may come and go; the flowers may bloom and fade; friends may pass from youth to age, or be held in the iron grasp of the destroyer; brothers and sisters may go away, and little baby faces spring up around them; their sweet baby lips may smile and prattle of the beauty of earth; the sun may rise and set, but she will not see it—the beauty of nature is a closed book to her. She is blind. Speak it slowly. Make no wild pretense of sympathy—you cannot see it—you cannot feel it as we do. "She is blind." We have so often heard these words and thought them so full of sadness ; but now they seem to hold worlds of meaning —darkness, despair, sorrow, pain, mental and physical suffering are all condensed into that one word, BLIND.

NOVEMBER 5.—Well if everything ended in a lifetime, I think I would like it ; if life would drift away from me to-day, I'd like it ; if I could just clap my hands together over my aching heart now, and crush its beatings—crush the pain out forever. I wish I could tie the strings of thought hard, tie them fast. I really am puzzled to find a solution to this problematic pain, for after all it is a problem to me ; it is a mystery.

I am not humble—that's a certainty ; and I never will be, I am wicked, I am rebellious, and I fight so hard that sometimes 1 grow too weary to know that the pain exists ; sometimes I am so indifferent that I feel like resorting to some strange penance to find out if it is I. And yet when I do up the frozen feelings, I find them so warm, so active.

I wonder if everybody else has such troubles as I do. I wonder if everybody else keeps a locked door behind which they hide some sorrow ; if they do, this is certainly a world filled with misery more than I believed it ; but then I know it is not true of every one ; I know it is not true that life has a superabundance of shadow.

JANUARY 7.—I have lived all these weeks in a

strange whirl of doubt and unrest, but somehow now the doubts seem less cloudy, less hideous, and a sort of calm is spreading over my heart. I have rebelled and complained, but I have been unjust and morbid. Slowly the justness of God's dealings is finding its way into my conscience and heart, and a calmer faith than three months ago I could have believed possible fills my heart and eases some of my mad pain. I have said it was impossible to believe what one could not see—impossible to believe what one could not understand ; but this is rank sophistry. When we see the roses blooming so beautifully we know that they must have had roots, they must have had health and vitality to have made a flower so perfect.

When we look at the dainty sweet smelling violet we know that an invisible power has been at work to fashion the flower so delicate and small—to imbue it with its fragrance and endow it with its beauty. We know this. What we see is the flower—we never hesitate to say it is a rose, a violet, but we do not see the roots ; yet if we are asked, we say we know they exist. But how do you know it ? Other roses have been examined and the roots found; therefore we know that to every flower is attached a root. Well, we say the violet is fragrant, we say we know it because it produces a pleasant impression on our sense; we have examined many violets, have inhaled their sweetness, have pressed them and crushed them and still found them sweet. We could not crush the sweetness out; we could not destroy it; yet we have never seen it. We have tried to analyze, tried to grasp it, but it has evaded us; still we know that it is there. How? We cannot see it, feel it, weigh or measure it, and the olfactory nerve is not strong enough to weigh against all the other faculties.

We say we love certain people—that they are congenial to us. We cannot analyze our feelings; we cannot measure our love, and yet we are sure that it is so; how it arises, we cannot tell; what gave it birth is a mystery past our finding out, and yet we know beyond all doubting that it exists. We feel its influence; we are governed by it in all our actions, and we cannot doubt it, for to doubt it is to lose desire for life; God is and yet we cannot see Him. We may try to crush out our loves, our hopes, our longings for the great good, but they exist truly as does the scent of the violet. None of these sentiments are palpable, none tangible, yet all exist.

We cannot prove the violet has no odor because we cannot see it. We cannot prove to other people that we love any one, yet we know it. We are more prone to doubt right things of late years than we were a quarter of a century ago, and more ready to grasp at the new, wrong faiths. Still there exists in every mind a half defined ideal of purity and goodness, which we call God; and no matter how hard we try, that faith in the supremacy of a mind never is eradicated. We cannot be materialists; no matter how hard we try, we will believe some things that we cannot see. God is, and doubts of this fact only make us more sensitive in our faith. When we doubt a good man's integrity and truth, and he is true to the core, there comes a half warning that we are mistaken, and we cannot urge ourselves into a perfect belief of his badness. The truth of his goodness is established in his own soul, and we cannot shake the faith of it out of our own minds. And whatever is truth will exist; and the efforts to put down the right only make us morbid and restless. Cold philosophy amounts to but little to the soul and heart; it touches the brain; it gives coolness in action, but it never gulls or reaches the truth that lies in the soul and heart. Life is a checker board on which God moves as King, and the hosts that surround Him are His knights and bishops.

CHAPTER III.

JUNE 1, 18–.—Another half-year has come and passed away since 1 wrote anything here. Change seems the order of the day all around. I have been into society some—I am learning men and women now, and finding that the world, taking it altogether, is pleasanter than I thought.

*   *   *   *   *   *

Here is an abrupt break in Maud's diary—her song of happiness is cut short, and there seems to be a shadow gradually creeping over her young life of trust. She is too bright not to make friends ; too good not to win love ; and her first intoduction into the world made her popular and a favorite. She had up to this time, except during a short period given in the last chapter, been the most trusting child I have ever known, but on the next page I find skepticism is taking root in her heart.

AUGUST.—Well, I am a woman now. Never again can I look with such trusting eyes into the future— never again can I build up such high castles of imagination as in my childhood days. It took me all those years to learn that I must not rely too implicitly on others—to learn that the world is not full of "my boys," and that I cannot have all love in this life. It has been a hard lesson too—a lesson difficult to master ; and has taken more time than I'd like to spend on many lessons ; but I hope there will be little necessity to spend so much time on anything else. Since I laid aside girlish pleasures and took upon myself some of the responsibilities of womanhood, I find everything around me assuming more realistic colors; more broad and decided shape. I see the things that have seemed play assuming the grand aspect of Duty. And yet, when I think of it, I have never known childish pleasure. Life has been an active drama for me from the first. It has been a battle all along. I am so constituted that work and action have seemed pleasure, and I have not had time to think of what was missing. I mean I have not known till now that childhood is past, and I have never been a child. When I think of all the strangely conflicting circumstances of my life—when I think that I have ever had the heart to laugh, it shocks me. I cannot understand that I have had any heart to smile. Truly, I was born to suffer.

Do you know that to-day as I sit here in the sunshine with this little book of Maud's in my hand it seems almost wrong to transcribe her girlish, outspoken sorrows—they were so sacred with her, so deep, so real; but I have a task before me, and I must gather all the links in this beautiful golden chain.

About this time a great quiet seemed to fall upon her. I could not fathom it; I could not understand why the gayety had fled; and her wise, womanly ways puzzled me, but she never spoke a word of sorrow or regret to me. It pained me inexpressibly to watch her day after day carrying on her face the shadow of a great grief. I have gone to her room when she was not expecting me and found her in tears—not such tears as we shed for those who die, or for a passing sorrow; but tears that lay deeper than death—do you understand me? I have seen her sit

for hours with her eyes (which were too bright from
much weeping) fixed on something I could not see;
and yet when she was with her mother she laughed
and sang, chatted and was gay. I saw that something
was being borne alone by my darling. One of her
brothers was away from home—the one she loved
best of all, but she never spoke of him to me as of
old. If I mentioned him, a sort of convulsion seemed
to take hold of her, but she would remain silent. I
naturally concluded that her trouble was something
concerning him, but if it was, she was too loyal to
him to tell it even to me. She had many friends, but
she was still my Maud—no other friendship came between us. True, there was one woman whom I always
distrusted, but whom Maud seemed to love—indeed, I
noticed that she was drawn toward this woman as if
by a spell.

It seems strange to me now, when I read over
Maud's little diary, how intensely, how deeply she
suffered, even as a child. She loved with the impetuosity of a southron, and suffered in proportion.
When she was only a little past seventeen I married.
I remember even yet the untold misery expressed in
her face on that morning. She—but you may read it.

JANUARY 21, 18-.—Kathie is married—married

to-day, and I am left alone, as I was years ago when I went to school for the first time. O, Kathie, Kathie, how I shall miss you! for never again will you be to me the sweet companion of my joys and sorrows—another has come between us. I know it is wicked and selfish, but I wish you had never met your Phillip; I wish we could have kept on as we have always done. If I were like Helen now I could make friends with some .one else; but I cannot; I have only you and I cannot, cannot give you up.'

JANUARY 23.—It seems to me that Kathie is dead; and yet I am not so mean as to wish her to neglect the love of her life for me, though I need and want her so. I think I would rather die than have her unfaithful in her new duties. A woman has no right to marry a man unless she loves him, and then nothing should ever come between them. I would have Kathie love Phillip as the one good thing in life. I would have her give him every confidence and make his life her own, for it seems to me of all God's ordinances, there is no other so holy, so beautiful, so binding as marriage; and I would not come between Kathie and Phillip—not even to save my heart from breaking. If ever I should love any man, I'll love him better than ever woman loved before—love him as my king, my sovereign, my lord, and nothing, no secret, no past wrong, no dark deeds shall ever divide us. Confidence and faith must be the watchword of married life. Ah, Kathie, I have lost, but I believe you have gained.

JANUARY 30.—Well, I am going out now and try my success at the wheel of fortune. I am tired of living so aimlessly. I must be at work. The children need educating and I must help them. I am young and strong and I must help the boys get a start.

FEBRUARY 2.—The way has opened. I am to be a country school teacher. Think of it! I, who have never been away from home, am going now to live among a new people and try a new work. It makes me feel almost old too. I am going to undertake this work; but God will help me, and I am anxious to get started. I want to feel that I am doing some good, be it ever so little. I want to feel that my life is not utterly wasted and useless.

ELSWORTH, July, 188-.—Well, I suppose I am settled, and to tell the truth I am not charmed. I find that this sort of life is anything but poetical and idealistic. Reality takes out the rose-colors of romance, and the teacher we read about who, by her beauty, her grace, her elegance and numerous accomplishments, wins all hearts, is not the teacher we meet in the country. I suppose I am a fair representative of the class, and anybody knows I am not up to the ideal standard, and I see little prospect of romance here. The people I board with are nice respectable, country people, who have a scorn of innovations, and look upon my simple toilet arrangements as foolery. I shall try in practicable ways to adapt my manners to their requirements, though I may find it a little hard at first; but I am not afraid of hardships, and I never shrink from difficulties. "Over the Alpine summit of great pain lieth thine Italy." I have been thinking how true this is. What an incontestable fact it is that " there is no excellence without labor," which means pain. Life's lessons are all hard, its paths all steep and rugged; though occasionally we find a nook on the roadside which invites us to rest. We may have traveled over many stretches of rocks to reach it, and when it is reached we cannot tarry long. The mandate is work, toil, endure. For over the mountain top you may see the gilded spires and glittering dome of your ambition—the Italy of your dreams; but it takes time, patience and strength to reach it. Go on. Keep the sunlight ever ahead. Leave the shadows behind. Look always to "Italy" and REST will come.

From this last passage I know that Maud's womanly growth was perfected. I know that life was becoming a stern reality to her and that she was learning more of trouble than I had guessed. Soon after she was settled in her new work she wrote, telling me of her surroundings and companions. I thought then, and I think now, that hers was a nature made for the most heroic sacrifices. I think I never knew so strange a mingling of the human and the divine as was noticeable in Maud. In the sun-

shine of life she was a very woman, with all a
woman's caprices, faults and coquetries, but when the
shadows stretched across the horizon, she was one of
the noblest, the grandest women that ever lived. Her
father was one of the best men I ever knew, and yet
one of the most unpractical. Many times ruin and
beggary seemed to confront him ; but at such times
Maud became the friend, the counselor and the support of his life—to-day a bright happy girl, full of
vague fancies and romantic dreams ; to-morrow a
quiet practical woman—a streak of sunshine in her
father's clouded sky ; a woman in whom the faculty
of tenderness was more fully developed than in any
one else I ever knew. I remember once we were
reading a newspaper paragraph entitled, " Natural
Mothers," in which the writer explained the nature of
motherly affection in this language: "There are
many women whose lives have never been blessed
with real motherhood, but are women whose lives are
perfect exemplifications of the true mother-woman ;
whose hearts go out in sympathy and love to all weak
creatures—to all suffering nature, and who know no
greater joy than that of caring for others " I think
if ever a woman fulfilled this description, Maud
Arnold did. Her whole life has been one of self-

abnegation. Many times I have rebelled for her—to think that she who is so nobly fitted for a life of perfect beauty should always have to tread rough paths. I never heard her complain, but I have known how her heart hungered for rest. Sometimes Helen Carton would bring me her letters to read. I give one here. It shows the dreamy poetic part of her nature, and the stern control she put upon her life. Helen loved Maud with a strong idolatry, and believed in her as the embodiment of all that was grand among women. When she received a letter from her she treasured it as something precious. In this we were alike and we spent hours talking of our dear friend and the letters which were so characteristic.

ELSWORTH, September 18, 188-.—Little Helen : I have finished reading your last letter. It has somehow served as a link between the past and me. It has recalled to memory the dear old scenes of my childhood, the bright hopes of my youth, the dreams of my infancy. I cannot tell how or why I have felt it all so deeply, but it is so. You know that sometimes a bird note or the tinkle of a bell, or perhaps the very sunshine reminds you of "a day that is dead,"—your fancy rushes back to a time long past. O Past ! O Youth ! we'd call you back to-day if we could

The other day I was hearing a reading lesson, and like a flash I was carried back to a day fifteen

years ago, when a little child, I said that same lesson
at my mother's side. I saw the butterflies in the
great rose tree at the window; heard the mocking
bird in the pear tree, and was eager for the lesson
to be ended that I might race after the butterflies.
It all seemed so vivid that I could scarce realize that
I was a woman of twenty-two and hundreds of miles
from the old home, teaching school for a bare sub-
sistence. O, Helen, I have learned some hard lessons,
haven't I? But I do not know that I regret them—
that is, I do not regret the knowledge and experience;
I only regret the learning; but it had to come sooner
or later; and the bitterest part is over.

And so you are going to put off your freedom
and buckle on the armor of matrimony—if you can
keep the same mind long enough; but, to tell the
truth, I sadly fear your knight will not win his spurs
after all, for you are a fickle maiden and have not yet
learned the lesson of constancy. But I will not write
you a long letter of advice and congratulation until I
know beyond a doubt that Helen Carton has merged
her existence into that of another. I know those
pretty eyebrows are drawn close together in dis-
pleasure at my outspoken skepticism, but never mind
—time will tell. Now smile and kiss me a loving
good-night, my dark-eyed maiden, and believe me
when I say I cannot get along without your love.

                                        MAUD.

Maud wrote to me often after this, telling me of

her work and her recreations. She was always an inveterate bookworm, and now her time was almost entirely spent among the poets. Her diary gives evidence of the impressions made by her reading.

April 9, 188–.—I have just put aside Dante's Inferno. The book has set my brain on fire. I am deeper in love than ever with the poets. They are gods. Poetry means to create. When from the beautiful volume of Thought springs a poem, a grand heroic strain of martial achievement and mighty deeds, we rejoice with a joy which is almost equal to that of the Creator. To us is denied the power, the beautiful gift of Song, but we catch the music and hear the echo in our hearts. The poets, God's Singers —they speak to us in rhythmical measure. They tell of joys which we cannot describe, but dimly feel. They tell us of a beauty which a painter cannot put on canvas. God bless the poets!—they live up higher than we. They live with "visions for their company," and yet we crush and cripple them. We clip their wings when they would fly. We hold them to the earth when they would soar to Heaven.

> "O world! that listens when too late,
> Unto the voice that sings,
> And loves the music when the years
> Have shattered many strings;
> But little owes the Bard to you
> For praises from your tongue,
> Who heard not when the Harp was new,
> And love and life were young."

"Poetry and art and knowledge are sacred and pure." Let man or woman try to dull the cravings, the ambitious longings of the brain and heart. These longings after the beautiful, the ideal infinity of learning, are not things of man's fashioning, but are impressions of God's own ideality of mental mechanism. He implants vast conceptions of truth in the brain, and if, to an overwhelming desire for the ability to give these conceptions wings, the circumstances of our life stand opposed; if the knowledge of our weakness. as opposed to the combined circumstances, comes, regret, despair and discontent are but natural; but they will pass away; for somehow an outlet will open after awhile, which will in a measure gratify one's ambition. But if we crush our impulsive longings, we crush out our soul; for all that is high and beautiful, all that is rare and lovely, emanates from God. and God works in the soul.

APRIL 12, 188–.—"The life that leads to Heaven, is not retirement from the world, but action in the world." To-day when I read this, it came to me as a pain, and I was angry that it had been written, for I knew that it was true; but it does not accord with my resolution, with my aims; and I am too selfish to want to do right, even if it conflicts with my preconceived ideas. I want to stay away from the world; I want to grow good in silence; I want to become beautiful in soul, alone. I have already seen too much of weakness, and am too weak myself to have any desire for further knowledge. Perhaps if I were stronger I should not feel so much the wrongs that others do. It may be I depend on others to maintain the good that is in me, and in doing this I am made aware of the bad in them. I think I have been a child till now—that I have felt as a child; but this can never be again. The child is dead—the woman lives. I have had confidence and given faith which has led to my undoing. I believed too much, and in believing, granted too much. Now I must live more and act less—must believe less and exact faith in myself. I wonder if I can live in the world, and act out a noble, pure, beautiful life; God grant I may.

> "Thou must be brave thyself,
>   If thou the truth wouldst teach;
> Live truly and thy life shall be
> A great and noble speech."

There is my answer. I, then, have been the wrongdoer. I have not been true and brave; and it is I who have taught others wrong; I have been the weak coward; I have made some one else act a lie— have led some one else along crooked paths. I never knew it before. I have blamed others for my wrong. I have condemned them as false when it was I who was false. I shall never be able to undo this wrong. I shall never be able to impress them with my truth again, and I cannot set them right any more.

APRIL 16, 188-.—What a dreary, sunless day; so full of foreboding trouble; so full of dim shadows and mocking hopes ; a day in which nature seems in harmony with my feelings. I do not believe nature feels the pain and grief of humanity. There certainly is a great deal of suffering about us, and God sees it all—nature is alive to our griefs. What a pleasant thought it is that God knows—that Nature feels! There are so many men and women around us who bear the heaviest burdens daily; but who hide them under a cloak of happiness—of borrowed smiles ! Aching hearts there are around us, and yet we laugh and are gay, as if in all God's universe there was naught but joy and hope. We fill up the measure of happiness after our own manner, as if there were no dead hopes, no aching hearts, no worn and weary feet. But, thank God! He knows, He feels, He cares.

APRIL 18.—I have just been reading a book of travels, and among the things which struck me the most forcibly is the description of an old church yard in which this inscription is traced on a grave stone :

HERE REPOSES
IN GOD,
CAROLINE DeCLEVY,
A RELIGIEUSE OF ST. DENIS,
AGED 83 YEARS,
AND BLIND.
THE LIGHT WAS RESTORED TO HER
IN BADEN,
THE 5TH OF JANUARY,
1839.

Just that and nothing more, and yet it is enough.

Grand, trusting faith—"light restored!" Think of it;
a life-long groping in darkness; wandering in the
valley of midnight—wrapped in a night of years.
Think of the life—think of the restoration. "A religieuse of St. Denis." There is the history of a life
in five words; a history of privation and tender min-
istration; of renunciation. A volume could not have
said more. A woman, tender, young and fair when
she began her work; aged, blind and weary when in
darkness it closed. Dead! Yes, forgotten by men
and women—passed out of existence, out of memory;
life's trials ended forever. No, there is nothing strange
in that. "It is but the common fate of all;" but
there is more. There is something beautiful, sublime,
thrilling in one little line of the epitaph which may
also be "the common fate of all:" "Light was restored to her." Here we have the history of a life;
the weariness, the pain, the darkness, the despair,
and, last of all, the compensation; rare, beautiful,
more priceless than gold—a recompense for every woe,
a reward for every good deed, a joy forever.

How that little word, blind, goes to my heart. I
feel that some link binds me to that past of hers,
which I never knew. Deep down in my heart I feel
the sorrow of hers, for I bear the sorrow of one that
is dearer to me than anything in the world. O my
dear little Paula, you are beginning now to learn the
weight of the burden you have to bear; but, thank
God, "light will be restored" some day—glorious,
everlasting light—infinite joy and peace.

* * * * *

Here comes a mighty jar, a terrible despair in Maud's life. One day this message reached her: "Come home; Paula is dying."

She came. I have seen women suffer, but I never saw such strong, relentless grief as hers, when she came and found her idol—dead, DEAD. When the great misfortune came to Paula, Maud was like one stunned; but after awhile came the relief in that life was left—she still had her darling's love and could exercise that beatific mother faculty for the dear one. But when the second stroke came, there seemed nothing left. One by one the links of happiness had been snapped, until now there remained so little;—and she was so hungry-hearted, so full of loving tenderness; yes, Paula was gone.

From that day I never heard her speak of her sister. She grew pale and thin and deeper sadness shone in her eyes than was natural. She went back to her work and worked to "still despair." I went to see her once and Paul went with me. He had never seen her since she was a child—that is, she seemed a very child to us. I never saw him so attracted by a face, as he was by hers; and somehow the sadness in her eyes crept into his. When we went home Phillip noticed it and asked me about it. I knew nothing, could tell nothing. Paul went away. He wandered from place to place, aimlessly, recklessly it seemed to me—I could not understand it.

Maud rarely wrote to me now. But once I received a letter when Paul was on a visit to me. I noticed that he was much agitated and left the room while I read it. When he came back I handed it to him. He never returned it. I was troubled more than I can tell at the change in him. Early in the spring of the next year, Maud's mother died, and she was again called home. Her grief at this time, though, terrible, brought about a favorable reaction. She saw now that her work was imperative ; and she was forced by stern duty to wear the semblance of a smile for her father's sake, and the effort brought its recompense.

CHAPTER IV.

After Maud comes back and is settled in the old house, the shadow seems to drift out of her eyes ; the burden on her heart seems lighter. Why ? Because Maud, my peerless Maud, is learning the lessons of love. Through years she worked and struggled for others ; planning and hoping and working for them,

with no time for selfish thoughts and girlish dreams,
living on merely a pittance of affection; for it is
always so; they who love deeply and unselfishly are
fed on husks, and rewarded with coldness. The girl's
heart had ached for warmth and sunshine, it had
pleaded for the beauty and glory of love, but plead in
vain. Some shadow would come between her heart
and its fruition, till a calm defiance settled on her
soul—a resolution to let happiness alone—to take
only what came and not to dream or hope. But this
resolution on her part was disastrous. She was young
and had an almost unlimited capacity for hoping;
and to give up life, to cease dreaming, was putting
too strong a curb upon her nature. A little longer
and she would have lost all the beauty of her character, all the sunshine of her nature, and all the
sweets of womanhood. But she came home to us,
and gradually the smiles crept back to her lips, then
to her eyes.

And Paul!—ah, my brother, that was a time of
perfect peace, and joy to you! I think from the time
he first saw Maud in that tiresome school room, he
loved her. Why he did not seek her and win her,
I cannot tell, unless it was that he depreciated himself and exalted her. Then perhaps the fact of her

girlish dislike and jealousy of himself had something to do with it. At any rate, he never sought her
out; but when fate or God placed her in his
pathway, he accepted the situation and improved it.
At first Maud was quietly indifferent and cold. But
little by little this changed; little by little her heart
melted, until I believe she was the most deeply
happy woman I ever knew. She never spoke to me,
she never told me; but I could see it, and feel it, and
it rejoiced my soul. Sometimes Phillip and I would
watch her sitting alone on the grass under the trees,
with her book or her work lying untouched in her lap,
with that beautiful, happy light in her eyes which
ever sent a thrill to my heart. Paul was my brother
and I loved him, I trusted him; but it made my
blood stand still, if for a moment the thought of the
possibility of his proving himself unworthy came to
me. I knew Maud, with her impetuosity, with her
deep, grand love, could not stand it. I knew that in
loving him, she believed in him implicitly; but that
with all her love, if he proved himself weak or unworthy, she would cast him from her heart, even if it
tore it to fragments; knew too that she had given to
him what she could never give to another; knew that
if he proved unworthy, she would forever cast him out

from her heart, and her nature would become warped into hideous misanthropy. Here is what she writes in her little diary :

MARCH 18, 188-.—To-day my life was given its crowning joy ; to-day the shadows dispersed, and the sunshine floods my soul. The clouds which have shadowed my pathway had a silver lining. Bless the Lord, O, my soul, and all that is within me, bless his holy name. How wicked I have been to doubt Him ! How wicked to think there was no God! and to feel like cursing the day of my birth, and longing for death. How cowardly I have been—weaker than I knew ; for I have been tempted to trifle with the life God gave me ; and now God, my Father, has been good to me as if I had always obeyed him. He has sent me joy and hope and love. O, God, forgive me, and blot my past sins from thy record and help me in the future !

*　　　*　　　*　　　*　　　*

O, Maud, Maud, how sweet was the hour of your happiness ! How beautiful the day of your sunlight! God pity us who hold the happiness of a human being in our hands ! God help us to be true and good !

The spring glided into summer—the dewdrops became roses and lilies and our Maud sang from morning till night—full of happiness, full of love and gayety. We fashioned the pretty dresses and dainty garments for our Maud's bridal. She would come to my sewing room sometimes and sit down on a little stool at my feet, and handle laces and edgings, not noticing them but watching me. One day she said ;

"Kathie, what are you making all these things for ?"

"My Maud, you little lady, you are going to be forced into society, dear, and you will find them all serviceable."

"Kathie, I shall not need them where I am going. Let them alone. God will take care of my future better than you can. Don't work on them, dear. I would rather have you talk to me."

"But, Maud, that is unnatural. You are only teasing me."

"No, I am not, Kathie. You may finish that white dress as soon as you please, but don't worry over the other things. Paul likes me in white, with lilies, and I want to wear them that day. I want you to make me look as beautiful as you can, Kathie; for I want him to remember me always as sweet and good and pure like the lilies, you know. He says I am the lily of his heart. He loves me very dearly,

Kathie, and I would have him hold me ever the true, pure, white lily—the snowy, snowy lily. Sometime, Kathie, he might unlearn some of the lessons he is learning now, you know; if I should ever be less good and sweet than he thinks me now,—and that would break my heart; so I shall not give him a chance. God shall care for me, and I shall always be the lily of his heart. Remember, Kathie, they must be those snowy, waxen lilies in the lower garden; not a bit of color in them. I think you will find them in bloom then."

She had never before alluded in any way to Paul's love for her or hers for him. It puzzled me, and there was something so quiet, so perfectly peaceful in her tone, that it made tears in my heart. She rose, kissed me on the brow, and went out. I sat for some moments thinking of her voice and manner, then took up the dress—a soft, snowy cashmere—and put all the finishing touches on it. But somehow, in spite of myself, the tears would fall. At last I folded the pretty white dress which our Maud was to be married in, and sat down and sobbed as if my heart would break. Five days later Maud came to my room with a bright light in her eyes, and said:

"O, Kathie, the lilies will be in time. There are

five which will be open in the morning. Now, don't forget them, dear."

And I did not. I can never forget the white lilies. In the morning we dressed our Maud in the snowy dress, with lilies at her throat, and in her hand, and then we called Paul. O, God! Thy will! But it was a hard, hard struggle.

"Paul, I can't tell it you, for my heart is all ready to break now!"

" She is dead! No more will her white fingers sweep
    The yielding ivory keys with rare, sweet grace;
No more will the glad, exultant, glorious soul
    Leap up with rapturous light into her face,
When through her parted lips flow forth rich waves of sound,
Till earth is made a heaven, with heavenly music crowned.

" She is dead! Never more will her fair hand pen
    Thoughts glowing with language quaint and eloquent—
Thoughts, which in the virgin soil of her pure heart
    All silently grew in sweet imprisonment,
To greet at last the heart's congenial who
Love what is good, ennobling, beautiful and true.

" She is dead! Never again will birds and flowers,
    And little children filled with wondrous love,
Feel the soft glance of her deep, haunting eyes.
    Radiantly tender, all other eyes above;
Or the delicate, gracious and caressing touch
Of her who here hath lost, but there hath gained so much.

"She is dead! The silver cord is loosed—
The earthen pitcher shattered at the fount—
The golden chalice broken and the pure soul
Hath plumed its flight to Zion's holy mount;
While we, who love her so, mourn her vacant place,
And yearn in vain, to gaze upon her angel face.

"She is dead! She tried to do her best
Within the narrow precincts of her daily life;
God's voice hath been her guide through weal and woe;
God's hand hath led her safely through this mortal strife.
Place this pale lily upon the saintly breast,
And leave her to her last and everlasting rest."

ONE CHRISTMAS EVE.

The flames leaped up brightly in the great wide-mouthed chimney, and the piled up hickory logs cracked and popped as if every fibre in them was strained to do duty on this Christmas Eve. A family of grown and half-grown children were gathered in the old-fashioned high-ceiled room, which, built in the early days of Kentucky, had done duty many years as "keeping-room." One small, plump, dark-haired girl, was comfortably seated on the rug, tying up wreaths of holly and cedar, to finish the festoon that was partly looped around the room, and her tongue was rattling along at electric speed, telling her brother about the grand party to be given at their nearest neighbor's on the ensuing evening.

"You know, Guy, that Mabel has just returned home, and Mr. Hill is going to kill three birds with one stone—that is, celebrate her home-coming, her birth-day and Christmas. It is to be a splendid affair,—do give me that bunch of holly, Fred, and—Dick, you go and break off a few more branches of cedar—O! Kate, isn't this lovely?" holding up a great cluster of berries and pressed autumn leaves. "Now, Guy, I want you to set your curls and brown eyes to captivate Mabel—Hattie, bring me the scissors, and don't take them away any more!—Kate, have you practiced that anthem? I hope papa will bring my box of flowers from town—".

"O sister! your tongue must need rest; and if you don't stop talking so fast and so much, you can't sing at all to-morrow;" and tall, handsome Kate, laughingly laid her hand over her sister's mouth. Elizabeth gave a clear musical laugh in response, and sprang up, saying:

"This is done, and now Guy, make yourself useful as well as ornamental—mount that ladder and hang this wreath for me—you can make your mark that high, if no higher, and your influence will be felt above us all !"

"Especially if he should fall back on us from his elevated position," said Dick.

The wreath was hung, the mottoes arranged, the chandeliers festooned with mistletoe boughs and holly, the litter cleared away, and the whole house, from garret to cellar, was in order. When the tea bell rang, the young folks, forgetting their dignity, went skipping across the wide old hall into the great dining-room, as if they were children. Even handsome Kate got off her "stilts," as Elizabeth called it, and allowed Guy to lead her into the room with most undignified rapidity. When they were all seated, the white-haired father asked a blessing, after which there was silence for several minutes broken only by the crackling of the logs on the fire and the chirp of the cricket. Then the father said :

"Well, my children, this has been a busy day with you, hasn't it ? and I expect you have planned to have a gay time to-morrow, especially as it promises to be a white Christmas, if it keeps snowing at the rate it has begun."

"Hurrah for the snow !" cried Dick, springing from his seat in his delight.

"O, I am so glad!" said Fred.

> " O, the snow!   The beautiful snow!
> Filling the sky, and the earth below—
> Over the house-tops, over the street,
> Over the heads of the people you meet;
> Dancing, flirting, skimming along,"

quoted Kate, and Elizabeth added:

> " The town is alive and its heart is aglow,
> To welcome the coming of beautiful snow;"

Then Guy repeated:

> " There's nothing so pure as the beautiful snow."

> " O, God! in the stream that for sinners doth flow,
> Wash me and I shall be whiter than snow,"

said the mother softly.

"Bravo!" said Elizabeth, "mamma has capped the climax."

"But then children," said their grandmother, who had been so quiet that for once she was forgotten, "there are little children that will suffer from the effects of the 'Beautiful Snow.'"

"That's true mother," said Mr. Weldon. "Every pleasure has some shadow of regret. I was thinking this evening that it has been twenty years since there were no little stockings to hang up in this home. My girls are all too big for that now. Last year Bertie's little stockings were to fill, but he's gone where there is a perpetual feast, and he is whiter than the "Beautiful Snow;" but, my children, suppose you take your baskets and go out and find some little stockings to fill."

There were tears in Elizabeth's voice as she answered :

"Yes, papa, we will go."

They were all somewhat saddened by the mention of the little darling that had gone out from them, and were ready to do this for his sake.

Though there was no moon, it was not very dark, for the white earth lent its light. Guy, with two baskets overflowing with good things ; Dick and Fred also well loaded ; Kate, with a basket filled with shawls and flannels ; and Elizabeth, according to her nature, with an assortment of everything—clothes for children of all sizes, shawls, edibles, toys, dolls, mittens, stockings, and, in fact, the largest bundle of all, stood in the hall, waiting for a hack to take their stores, each a little quieter than usual. Their grandmother came out with a large paper box, saying :

"Here, children, is my offering, and God bless your gifts !"

Elizabeth raised the cover, and exclaimed joy-ously :

"O, grandmamma, how welcome they will be to some cold feet this freezing weather,—see, Guy, there are two dozen pairs of socks. Isn't she too good?" she said kissing her grandmother rapturously.

"Who made all the little garments in that basket, Bessie?" said grandma, with a kindly sparkle in her eyes.

"O, but grandma, I am young, and ought to do it—besides, Katie did as much as I—but wasn't it splendid of papa to think of our taking these things to-night instead of waiting till morning? Ah! here is John with the hack—let's put the baskets and bundles in and we will walk."

There was not a house in the village, where poverty reigned, that was not visited that night; and not a little heart in the community that did not beat with happiness the next morning; and every man, woman and child that could leave home, was at church; and every heart, if not every voice, joined in the anthem, "Peace on earth, good will to men."

The sweet face of the Madonna smiled down on the group gathered in Mr. Weldon's parlor Christmas evening; and Elizabeth was standing just under the

chandelier and looking up at a new picture to which
a card was attached, bearing the simple inscription
"To Miss Elizabeth Weldon," when Henry Clinton
stepped to her side and breaking off a bunch of holly
and mistletoe, said:

"Miss Bessie, do you know the forfeit for being
caught under the mistletoe?"

Elizabeth blushed and stepped aside quickly,
saying:

"If I am caught there again, I will pay the
forfeit."

"And," said he, "if I catch you there again, I
will hold you strictly to your promise and ask you
for another."

"THEY MET BY CHANCE."

The mellow light of an April morning crept
through the latticed window of a modest little
chamber in a modest little cottage on the outskirts
of a pretty village in the sunny land of Florida, and
rested for a few moments on the dark hair of a
young man; then shifted its position so that it lay
upon his face, and caused him to open wide his brown

eyes. He pushed the fleecy blanket from his breast, and said impatiently :

"I have overslept myself again, and she will not come any more until to-morrow, and so I must wait. It is strange she seems to avoid my seeing her at all. I almost dread the prospect of my recovery, for then I will have to leave this little Eden, and of course leave Eve behind."

There was no one in the room save the sick man when he awoke, but as he ceased speaking a pleasant little woman of perhaps forty-five entered and approached the bed, and bending almost tenderly over the sufferer, brushed back the rich, clustering hair, and bathed the feverish brow. She moved about putting things to rights, and then seated herself in an easy chair beside the bed and began to arrange some fresh flowers in a little basket filled with moist sand to prevent their withering. The invalid had not stirred, and Mrs. Benton thought him sleeping; but just as she was putting the last flowers in the basket he said :

"Will you not tell me who it is that brings those flowers every morning ? She always comes before I am awake and I cannot see her."

"How do you know then that it is a woman ?

and what reason have you for believing any one beside myself ever enters your room?" answered the lady with a merry twinkle in the soft gray eyes.

"You have been very kind and good to me ever since I came here, and I am very, very grateful to you for what you have done; but I know I am not deceived in thinking that there is another that sometime visits my room; I know that it is no mere fancy picture that floats through my mind, but a reality; and it is not imagination that leads me to believe that another form than your own sometimes stood beside my bedside when I was so sick and feverish; I know that somebody else used to hold the medicine to my lips, some one else used to pass two little white hands over my head when the fever scorched it so terribly; and though I have never seen that pretty vision since I came back to consciousness, yet if ever I do see her I will know her. Already I love her, and if she will not let me see her, please thank her for her kindness to me."

"Well, well! You are an imaginative creature; here you are trying to act over the part of Waverly and Rose Bradwardine. You have no reason for believing that anyone besides myself and Jane enters your room—but never mind; you will soon be well, and then you may try to find this fairy vision. Would you not like to have this pretty white rose-bud ? It is the first I have seen of the kind this year, and you seem so fond of flowers that I know you would like it; but it is almost time for your breakfast now, and I am going to prepare it for you. While I am gone I want you to breathe this fresh April air; it will give you a good appetite."

The lady rose and opened the windows, thus letting in a broad belt of sunshine, and then left the room. While she is gone I will tell you who our hero is and how he came here. His name is Robert Clifton. He is the son of a Southern planter whose fortunes are on the ebb, and he has gone into the world to fight the battle against poverty. He had worked hard all the year, and his health suffered so from confinement that at last he was compelled to take a holiday; and, as his purse was slim, he determined to go to some quiet, out-of-the-way-place, to build up his wasted strength, and had chosen this little cottage among the flowers of Florida. Scarcely had he reached his place of destination before his strength gave way entirely, and he was prostrated by a terrible fever. For two weeks he has been a prisoner within this little room; but now he is recovering, and his physician says he will soon be on his feet again.

He mended rapidly, and a week later was able to sit up, and even to walk about the garden; and in a short time into the fields, growing stronger and more robust every day. He had never given up his belief in the existence of his fair nurse, and in all his rambles he was ever hoping to meet her, but had been disappointed.

One day while on a hunt he chanced to take a new direction, and had gone much farther than usual when he was suddenly brought to a halt by a fence which he supposed, from the neatness of the smooth-shaven grasses and the well-trimmed trees, enclosed an old fashioned country lawn; but he wondered that the place was so neatly kept. Suddenly he determined to find out what it was, so he bounded lightly over the fence, and pursued his way among the tall beautiful trees. The dark green leaves of the water-oaks, interspersed with magnolias which were in full bloom, and the green pines that stood majestically beside some young bays that had not as yet reached the dignity of mature years—all combined to form a very pretty and fascinating picture. Robert took all this in and seemed to enjoy the freedom which he felt

here in this grove as much as a school girl of fifteen
would have done after a confinement within the brick
walls of a boarding school for a year; and he enjoyed
it from a higher sense of understanding. He saw in
all this beauty the hand of a divine Workman, and
it was with a feeling of reverence that he walked on
through the grove. Directly he came to the top of
the hill and looked down into a pleasant little valley.
Here was an artificial lake, around it growing the
broad-leafed water-lily; and across it was stretched
an artistically-constructed bridge. A woman, with a
large sun-bonnet drawn forward, leaned over the rail-
ing. She held a book of blue and gold in her gloved
hands, and gazed down into the water with a far-
away, dreamy look in her eyes. She seemed very
much entertained by her thoughts; and they were
evidently very pleasant ones, for suddenly she threw
back the bonnet and laughed a merry, girlish laugh,
so full of happiness that you would have trusted her
immediately; for no one could have been deceitful
whose laugh gave out such a clear, musical, innocent
ring as did hers. She turned to pick up her bonnet
which had fallen to the ground, when her clear blue
eyes met those of Robert Clifton bent eagerly and in-
quiringly upon her. She was evidently very much

confused, for a rich crimson swept over the transparent, colorless face, and she hastily hid it in the friendly shade of her bonnet; but the confusion passed away almost as quickly as it came, and she started forward saying .

" I was not expecting to see you this morning, Mr.—." She suddenly stopped, and the deep tide again swept over her pretty face.

"So you are my nurse—I am so glad, so glad to meet you ! And now you must tell me your name. I have wanted to see you, and tell you how much I thank you for your kindness to me during my illness. I never saw you with the eyes of clear consciousness, but I knew you just now, and should have known you had I seen you across the seas. Again, let me thank you."

She held out her little white hand, from which she had removed the large, loose bleaching gloves, and said :

" I see you do not remember your old playmate ; I am Kathie Miller, and when I was a little thing you used to know me well enough, but I guess now that I have grown up I must have changed, and perhaps I do not look like the little red-headed girl you used to take along with you everywhere you went."

"Why, indeed is it Kathie? I should never have known you for the same little girl I used to think so much of—may I take up the acquaintance where I left off?"

"O yes; for I am not at all disposed to be formal, and papa says I never will be a woman; but I used to like you, and I don't see why I need make like you are a stranger now—only may be I will not like you as well as I did when you were a boy; for I believe men are like us—they change as they grow older; though I don't see that I am changed in anything, only that I am not quite so ugly as I used to be! My hair is ever so much prettier, and even I cannot call it red; and then those great ugly freckles are not half so bad. Do you not think I am improved?"

Robert smiled at the young lady's quaint, innocent speech, though he could not detect a particle of vanity in her tone, and he answered her accordingly. He did not flatter, but gave his opinion of her personal attractions in such a manner that she felt he meant what he said. And now, why need I prolong the story? Is it necessary to tell of the courtship and final result—of the bridal dresses and of Robert's success in life? Of how he rises higher and higher in the world's estimation, ever winning laurels? Of how Kathie is the same innocent, trusting woman; and how completely she holds the hearts of her husband and children in her keeping? Her work in life is now in its prime, and she is going on and on. Never a sun goes down that it has not witnessed some good done by this noble woman. If ever she grows tired, she has but to retrospect. Her work is nobly done, and her

"Firm tread on life's track
Will come like an organ note, lofty and clear,
To lift up her soul and her spirits to cheer."

IN EXTREMIS.

CHAPTER I.

Somewhere among the hills just outside of the noise and bustle of the city, is nestled a little farm, with sloping undulations on all sides. The fields are under the best of cultivation; the horses are thoroughbreds, and the cows are the gentlest and sleekest. There are no fences down, no gates swinging on broken hinges. Every thing about this little home speaks of comfort and plenty.

As you approach the pretty Gothic cottage which shows fitfully through the trees, you cannot repress the home feeling which comes over you; the birds carol so sweetly in the great elms and poplars which meet above your head ; in the distance you hear the clear call of the plow boy and the deep bay of the dog just beyond the hills. As you approach nearer the house, you hear the hum of the busy bees, as they gather honey from the myriads of brilliant flowers. Presently with other familiar sounds is blended the full clear tones of a woman's voice, as she accompanies herself on the piano. She is singing the dear old song which for years has made a part of our pleasant recollections of the old home—a song which our mothers used to sing in a sweet tender voice, which perhaps we will never hear again. Suddenly the song ceases, and a glad, merry, girlish voice breaks in with :

"O, Rachel, Rachel, I have two of the jolliest little white kids you ever saw ! Papa bought them from Ed Holt, and I've put them in the meadow. Now, do come and see them. They are just too cunning for anything !"

Rachel, a dark-eyed, dark-haired little woman, somewhat fleshy, but well proportioned, rose from the piano, and with an affectionate smile, followed the girl who, too eager to walk quietly, catches her com-

panion's hand and hurries, half walking, half running into the yard, and turning to the left, approaches
a field of blooming clover, where the cows are quietly
browsing. The girl, not heeding the gate, takes a
running start, leaps over the low fence in true boyish
fashion, and before her sister has entered the gate
is back again, with the little, creamy, Cashmere kids
in her arms, and a proud, exultant look in her gray
eyes, exclaiming :

"Aren't they beauties, Rachel ? Will they hurt
the flowers ? I do hope not, for I want them to run
in the yard—they are too pretty to put off here with
the calves, and then they might get hurt. I'm going
to name one of them Alma, for that girl papa read us
about yesterday, who was so white and pure that the
people worshipped her ; and the other I'll call Paul—
O no ! I'll name them Paul and Virginia."

The momentous question of a name being settled,
the little foster mother fell to caressing her pets. Her
long straight black hair which was a ceaseless tor-
ment to her, fell like a veil over the wee white kids.
There was something indescribably graceful and
charming in the girl's attitude and motions, and her
elder sister, noticed it, with an expression of face half
smiling, half sad; but had she been asked the cause of

the emotion of sorrow, she would have been unable to give an answer. Some things there are which impress us strangely, and seemingly without cause, and yet if we would trace out on the pages of the after-life the history of these things, we would find that the impressions are seldom deceptive. I think the spirit penetrates regions unknown to reason, and grasps some of the most powerful truths of our lives or the lives of others.

Rachel was the eldest daughter of this family, and had been a mother to this "Gypsie lassie." I think she scarcely loved her own little ones more than this motherless sister, whose babyhood she had guarded—the child who had been a mother's parting gift.

But the sun was going down, and Rachel roused herself from the reverie into which she had fallen, and called her sister to come in doors. She was met on the threshhold by a negro girl bearing in her arms a beautiful boy of eighteen months, who called gleefully to his mamma to take him. She held out her arms, and the little fellow sprang into them, nestling his curly brown head on her neck. A door opened at the end of the long wide hall, and two other children came in with happy faces and sweet childish words, to kiss and love the dear, pretty little mother who never turned away from them, but joined merrily in their sports, forgetting that twenty-five summers had kissed her brow with loving lips.

Rachel Audly was one of those women whose happiness was bound up in the sweet home joys; whose life demanded no wider field, no higher position than the blessed one of wife and mother. Her children were her jewels, and treasured beyond the value of gold, till there was nothing narrow in her nature. Her husband spent most of his time upon the sea, but she and her boys never failed in their prayers to remember "the dear one whom God keepeth while away."

After a little time spent in gay frolic with the children, they were joined by their grandfather, whose brow bore the finger-marks of sixty winters. His appearance on the long piazza was a signal for a general stampede in his direction, the children leaving their mother and rushing to him. They climbed into his lap, one perched upon his shoulder, another on his knee, while the little one nestled in his arms, laughing in true baby fashion at the sport; the mother standing at his side, with one hand supporting the boy on his shoulder, the other laid caressingly about his neck.

"Where is the little elf, daughter ?"

"I don't know; she was with us a minute ago. Perhaps she has gone to superintend the arrangements she ordered to be made for the accommodation of her pets."

"Bless the child! she is fond of that class of pets; so was her mother, and she is growing more and more like her every day."

"O, here she comes !" cried the eldest of the boys, springing from his grandfather's knee. "My ! but aunt Mamie, what are they ?—will they bite ?"

"Will 'em bite ?" echoed the second boy, taking a position beside his brother.

"No, Robbie, they won't bite," said the girl, replying to the last speaker. "Don't you see how gentle they are ? and they are mine, but I'll let you all come and see them when they get to keeping house. They will move into their house to-morrow, I guess, and we'll have a party then; but we must all take them something to begin house-keeping on, just as they did when Mr. Roland and his wife moved into the new parsonage."

"I'll take my little stool that Hal made for me," said Henry, the oldest, speaking up valiantly.

"And I'll tate 'em my—my pop dun," said Robbie, whereat Henry said scornfully:

"What will they do with a pop-gun to keep house on?"

"Den I'll tate 'em my 'ittle boodle," said Robbie after a pause, trying to think of something he could give, and his bugle being his dearest treasure next to his pop-gun.

"O that won't do either," said Henry.

"Yes it will, for they can blow it for a dinner-horn," said grandpa, whereupon Robbie hid his happy face in his mother's lap, and Henry for an instant looked crestfallen.

"Well, I guess I'll have to give them something, too," said the mother,—"what shall it be, Elfie?"

The girl looked up laughing, and said:

"O I guess you had better give them a stove. Papa thinks as he gave the housekeepers that he has nothing to do with the house, but we won't let him off that way—he must buy collars with their names on them. So you see, you stingy old man, we claim something more from you," and she gave him a kiss.

"Well, you little Elf, but I was waiting for an invitation to the party."

"I thought you disliked formality," said the girl, a ughing. 'Now behold how consistent is man," and she gathered the little kids in her arms and ran around the corner, singing as she went.

The father smiled fondly, and turning to Rachel said :

"She's a bright little Elf, isn't she, dear ?"

CHAPTER II.

Perhaps I have introduced Major Weston's family a little unceremoniously, and the Major insists that he hates (?) ceremony.

Easton Hill has been for many years one of the most charming homes in all the "blue grass regions." Its proprietor, Major Weston, an officer in the late war, is a gentleman of cultivation and refinement, and though by no means wealthy, yet by prudence and good judgment, he manages to live in a charming style, and to surround his family with many of the elegancies of life. When his country demanded his services, he gave up quiet life, and with his four sons who were just budding into manhood, went into the army. Two of his boys, the oldest and the youngest, fell in battle, one at Manasses, and the other at Gettysburg; and when the struggle was over, and the father returned, he left them sleeping the last sleep of brave men who have fought and died for their coun-try. The father never murmured against fate for taking them from him, for they had fallen at their post of duty, and he could ask no more. That he mourned is certain, but he would not let his grief darken the days that remained to him, but took up his old occupations, and put his farm in order, as in happier days. His remaining sons married and went their separate ways in the world, building up happy homes of their own. His daughters, Rachel and Naomi, also married, but continued to dwell in the home of their father. Rachel's husband was a sailor, and when he was away it seemed best that she should remain in the old home which could ill afford to lose her. Naomi married a civil engineer who was also necessarily away much of the time; and so the father kept both of his daughters, and the little children that came were as tokens of God's love to the soldier's heart, and he lived over the old days when, a young husband, he first came to Eston; and his grandchildren were to him as his own little ones.

And then he had Mary, his heart's idol, the ewe lamb of the flock, his last born, his Joseph—for of them all he loved this little one best.. The mother had been a sacrifice to this child, for when the wee lassie opened her baby eyes, it was not to find a smiling mother, but a weeping father. He called her Mary—for was she not born out of bitterness and trouble? Mary— bitter; how prophetic! How significant of the life which the future held in store for her. From the hour she was born the father had opened his heart to her, and given her such a wealth of affection as few children ever get; but there was no jealousy of the household pet, the little queen whose demands were never disregarded by her loving, loyal subjects. Even her brothers, when, with their families they visited the old home, petted and caressed her as no other child ever was petted and caressed. They tried to spoil her. They put her in the high places, and called her "queen," but for all this, she grew up as other children—no better, no worse; but simply a child, with all a child's impulses and excellences of character as other truthful children have.

* * * * *

Four years passed by on slippered feet, when a discordant note broke the perfect harmony of the melody—one link dropped out of the chain. Mr. Audley, Rachel's husband, was lost at sea, and for many days there was sorrow and weeping in the old home. And, illustrative of the old saying that troubles never come singly, just as the bitterness of grief was wearing away, a terrible fever broke out in the neighborhood; Naomi and her father were stricken down, and in less than one week, having finished their work on earth, they were laid to rest. The father left behind him the record of a well spent life. The daughter had scarcely laid aside girlhood's joys for womanhood's duties, and gathered a few golden sheaves, when the willing hands were released, and the spirit called home. It was bitter, very bitter, but the cup was not yet empty. Next, Naomi's beautiful twins were stricken down and died, and then Rachel's eldest boy. The clouds darkened the whole horizon, and the "days were dark and dreary." Naomi left one child, her eldest, a golden-haired, bright-eyed girl, whose beauty had always been something remarkable; and Mary, whose heart was bursting with its weight of woe, took the little Ethel to her bosom with eager love. The days never hurried now, but dragged by on lagging feet—time had grown tired of haste. Rachel, widowed, and deprived of one of her children, seemed a weary, aged woman. Her pale face seldom kindled up with smiles now, for her heart was crushed, broken. Naomi's husband went abroad —too weary to stay at home and be forever mocked by the joys that "were dead," he became a wanderer in a strange land. So Rachel and Mary, with the children that were spared, remained in the old home. But even the little ones seemed to have grown grave, for they seldom laughed as children are wont to laugh; and in vain they watched the faces of their aunt and mother for smiles, or other tokens of returning happiness. Happiness! O what a mockery in the mere word! Can happiness come to broken hearts? Can joy shine up through the deep grave of buried love? When clouds are dark, do we think of silver linings or golden lights? If it were so, hope would drive away sorrow, and silence despair; but we never dream of the golden light till we catch a faint glint of its brightness.

The deep sea of sorrow overwhelmed Rachel, and every note of joy but added to her pain. The words of this sweet old song sank deep into her heart:

" When swallows build, and leaves break forth,
My old sorrow wakes and cries;
For I know there is dawn in the far, far north.
And the scarlet sun doth rise;

Like a scarlet fleece the snow-field spreads
　　And the icy founts run free,
And the bergs begin to bow their heads
　　And plunge and sail in the sea.

" Oh! my lost love, and my own, own love,
　　And my love that loved me so;
Is there never a chink in the world above
　　Where they listen for words from below?
Nay, I spoke once and I grieved thee sore—
　　I remember all that I said;
And Now thou wilt hear me no more, no more
　　Till the sea gives up her dead.

" We shall walk no more through the sodden plain,
　　With the faded bents o'erspread;
We shall stand no more by the seething main,
　　While the dark wreck drives o'erhead;
We shall part no more in the wind and rain,
　　Where our last farewell was said;
But perhaps I shall meet thee and know thee again
　　When the sea gives up her dead."

CHAPTER III.

CLOUDS.

" And naught can bring from the happy past,
　　When light and love are fled,
Tho' the walls of the dear old home may last,
　　But memories of the dead."

The wind blew lightly across the room, fluttering
the snowy curtains, and bringing in sweet odors from

the wild, luxurious garden which lay half buried behind a tangled hedge of Cherokee rose. This old garden had once been well trimmed, well tended, and showed that busy, tasteful hands had cared for it; but now, ah! now, it is a wild waste of overgrown flowers, and not a "breath of the time that had been," hovered about it; for the hands that tended it are folded, the hearts that loved it are cold, and the days that were bright with their presence, are gone forever. But the wind takes no heed of all this, as it sweeps the petals of the roses down, and sends their breath, like sweet incense, into the old rooms; it takes no heed that it is stirring old memories, as it wakes the sleeping flowers; it takes no heed that to one patient, suffering heart, it is bringing back the memory of "a day that is dead"—that the breath of roses, honey-suckles and violets, is filling the chambers of Memory with sad, tender regrets.

A pale, black-robed figure sits patiently stitching a long, tiresome seam, trying to still the tumult which the wind and flowers have raised; never pausing to let the tears fall, but bravely pressing them back. A sudden gust of the frolicsome wind comes through the open window, lifts her work to her face, sweeps a paper from the table, and overturns her basket. Then she clasps her slender, nervous hands, closes her eyes, and gives way to the spell which the wind has wrought. She goes back over the bright, bright past, and revels in its beauty and sunshine. Again she is a child, running wild and untrammeled, over the great fields of wheat, tossing the yellow plumes right and left, and watching the shy partridges as they fly away at the sound of her merry shouts. Again, hatless, and with flying hair, she is mounted on her beautiful, black Lodi, and careering over the country, winning the disapprobation of the staid, prudish old women, and the hearty cheers and warm friendship of the boys and men. Anon, she is perched on a limb of the old horseapple tree, back of the garden, with a book in her hand, half-reading, half-dreaming, with the whisper of leaves in her ear. Again her thoughts turn to later years, when she had grown into a tall, slight girl, and merry voices filled the now quiet home; when childish feet danced in and out, and music and laughter were heard all the day. But now—O what a change! The youth and joy are gone—the childish voices are hushed forever—the tender, loving hands once so strong and active, are at rest. Good-bye, sweet, sunny days! Good-bye, childhood and hope! Ye are but a dream that is past—a rose that has been gathered. The winds cannot stir the past into life, try they ever so hard ; they can only waken memory and regret. Ah ! well, perhaps it is better so.

" After the shower, the tranquil sun;
Silver stars when the day is done;
After the snow, the emerald leaves;
After the harvest, golden sheaves.

" After the burden, the blissful meed;
After the furrow, waking seed;
After the flight, the downy nest;
Over the shadowy river, rest."

CHAPTER IV.

SUNSHINE.

Far out in the east a crimson streak of light shoots across the leaden horizon, a pale flush of pink spreads gradually over sky ; the birds awaken from their night of silence, and twitter and chirp as they flit among the dew-laden branches. Now the pink flush deepens, the great round ball of fire comes up and brightens the whole earth, the twitter of birds swells into song. The night of restless dreams and boding fancies is past ; its sorrows are buried in the mists of receding time, or only stand as sign-posts along the road of yesterday, and the glad new day is born.

The sorrows of the past, though buried, are not forgotten ; but they may be covered over with sweet fresh flowers, whose fragrance smothers the scent of the wormwood and gall. Perhaps sometime when the flowers are faded, and turned to ashes, the old sorrows may revive to mock with their skeleton arms and ghostly presence ; but little reck we of future trouble, if the sky of the present is fair. Mary Weston sees no shadows before her now—they all lie in the past. It all seems a hideous dream, and yet a real one. She knows that her heart contains many buried hopes ; she knows that her life has been rough and rugged, and beset with thorns. But the winds of time have swept across the graves of her buried hopes, and covered them with leaves amid which the grass is springing. They have ceased to be dark hillocks of unsightly clay, but have become fair mounds of verdure and blossom. To her, each hillock represents an angel in the skies ; and there is no longer pain in the thought that her loved ones are gone, for they have gained immortality. There is no pain in the thought that for them life's trials are over, but rather, it seems well that God has called

them home. Other griefs have come to her since the
first wave of sorrow swept over her soul, other lives
been gathered unto God, other links added to her
golden chain of angel loves. Rachel has gone to
meet her husband and children. She lingered for a
time after they were gone, but homesickness for the
little ones drew her away. She sighed :

> " I pray you what is the nest to me—
>   My empty nest?
> And what is the shore where I stood to see
>   My boat sail down to the west?
>
> " Can I call this home where I anchor yet,
>   Tho' my goodman hence hath sailed?
> Can I call this home where my nest is set,
>   Now all its hope has failed?
>
> " Nay! but the port where my sailor went—
>   The land where my nestlings be;
> There is the home where my thoughts are sent—
>   The only home for me."

And so she drifted out with the tide, and now
her boat is anchored in the heavenly port.

Mary has struggled with the world—has gone
into its highways and byways of trouble, but God
has helped her. He loves His little ones, while He
chastens them, and when the waves beat high, He is
ever at the helm.

When Mary Weston's life had grown almost barren of purpose, when the hopes of her girlhood had perished, God sent her friends and she began to form new plans for her life. What a blessing it is that we are endowed with an unlimited capacity for loving. When we bury one love, another rises, if not to fill the vacant place, at least to give interest and purpose to life.

After a time a lover came to woo the quiet, gentle woman, who was devoting her life to the suffering and sorrowing. His life, like hers, had been touched with sorrow and disappointment, and he knew how to feel for her loneliness. They walked along the shaded lanes together, as they went to minister to the sick, he as physician, and she as sympathiser and worker. She saw him, gentle, kind, thoughtful. He saw her sweet, womanly, Christ-like, moved by a spirit of faith and love that was inimitable, and his heart went out to her ; and almost before she knew it, she once more began to take some pleasure in life. Music again found its way to her soul, and floated out in her sweet, rippling, melodious voice. The days no longer dragged, but seemed all too short for her happiness. Love was stirring the depths of her silent heart never to be silent again. The love that came to her was involuntary. God sent it, and there were no doubts and fears to disturb her when she gave her heart and hand into the keeping of Robert Leighton.

CHAPTER V.

Once more we turn to the early home of Mary Weston. The old house has undergone many changes, and yet it is recognizable as the beautiful home we first looked upon years ago, when Mary was a happy, light-hearted girl. Time has only added beauty to the old place, and to see it now you would scarcely dream that sorrow had ever darkened the doors of this Arcadian home. Beautiful roses clamber over the lattice and creep in at the open windows. The whole yard is one mass of color and fragrance. From the piazza, which overlooks the orchard, you can see men and boys at work loading wagons, with the gold and red apples, while childish figures run here and there under the trees where the apples are thickest, shouting with merriment when one strikes them on the head, and each trying to see who will catch the most while they fall. Presently a sweetfaced woman, with a broad-brim straw hat on her head, comes out of the door leading to the orchard. Happiness and contentment light up her face, and sweet, mother-love sparkles in her eyes. When the children see her they dart away from the trees to some secret hiding place, and taking out a nice apple that had been saved for " mamma," they run to meet her, laughing joyously. The mother stands with outstretched arms to catch them as they come.

"See, mamma, see the nice apples we have saved for you," they exclaim in a breath.

"Yes, my darlings, but haven't you saved any for papa?"

" O, you must save some for him, for we couldn't tell which to give the nicest to, for we love you both alike."

The mother stooped and kissed them. Just then, a grave, yet pleasant looking man joins the group; but when the children begin to pelt him with apples, his face lights up with amusement and he enters into their sports with a will. Presently the children return to the wagons, and as her eyes follow them, the mother takes her husband's hand and says:

" It is a blessing to live, isn't it, Robert?"

" Yes, dear, but a greater blessing to love," he says, stooping to kiss the sweet mouth.

These two have just reached the meridian of life, and the sorrows of their early years lie far behind them. Mary Leighton is happier in her womanhood, than Mary Weston was in her girlhood. The seed-time was dreary and unpromising but the harvest-time is rich with golden fruits.

There are blessings in store for all if they will be patient and wait. A bow of promise spans every sky, and hope may illume every heart. The road of life may be rugged, and the clouds dark, but there is always the hope of a "sweet bye and bye."

TO-MORROW.

"To-morrow is a satire on to-day, and shows its weakness."
—[YOUNG.

" What name doth joy most borrow
When life is fair?
To-morrow.

What name does fit best sorrow,
In young despair?
To-morrow."
—[GEORGE ELIOT.

The clouds have gathered thick and dark over the heavens, the sunlight is dimmed, and no strug-gling ray of light comes through ; the clouds are so dense that they have dimmed all the glory of the sunlight—have hushed all the sweetness of song, and

life is sad.　All day you watch the clouds for one rift
in the darkness; for one stray beam of light; for one
bright spot to build hope upon; but you see no light,
and the darkness is deeper, and you console yourself
with the thought that there is a silver lining, and go
to sleep dreaming of—to-morrow.　To-morrow it will
surely be brighter.　The sun cannot always remain
behind the clouds.　But to-morrow dawns, and fades
out, and happiness stands afar off; but there will be
another to-morrow, and again you go to sleep dreaming of the day that is coming.

God never gave a mortal more than he could
bear, and if you are not a coward, you will not give
up, but work.　Some one has wisely said that "action
is man's salvation," and he who mopes, and gives
himself up to vain hopes of the to-morrow, cannot be
happy.　To-morrow is one of the beautiful unattain-
ables, and makes us ever hopeful; but to-day is with
us, and "time runs waste," let the watchword be.　Act
in the living present, and when to-morrow comes, the
measure of good deeds will be heaped up and overflowing.

> " Make the path thy feet shall press
> 　Smooth for those who follow,
> That their toilsome feet may press
> 　Every hill and hollow."

The actors of to-day will leave their impress upon the world ; and though they do not live to see the to-morrow, their deeds and words will. Pope, in beautifying his grounds, had not merely the gratification of his own tastes in view. He wrote to a friend : "They will indeed live after me, but I am pleased to think my trees will afford fruit and shade to others when I shall want them no more."

Fill up life's to-day with actions which will ring clear of reproach in the future. Bring fruit of perfect mould and without blemish, as your offerings, and God will insure the reward. If your life is a wreck, who made it so ? God ?

We read of "might have beens," of "hopes lost," of opposing "fates," and a great deal of nonsensical rubbish ; but let fate and circumstances be what they may, there is always an alternative, and he who gives up at the first touch of adversity, will not have known how to appreciate prosperity. If fortune frowns on one side, turn somewhere else. The road for your feet is somewhere—find it ; and leave an influence that will tell on—To-morrow.

BEAUTIFUL VALLEY.

In the Beautiful Valley, is a garden in which are all of nature's loveliest and choicest fruits and flowers. The sun shines down on this garden with a softer light than it does elsewhere, or so it seems to those outside, for it is never too warm—and never too cold ; the dews are heavier and the rain milder than anywhere else in the world; the streams are clear and ripple over pebbly bottoms with soft murmurs; the sea, as it lashes the shore at the foot of the garden, sends forth music like that of the Eolian harp. "And no storms ever beat on that beautiful shore in the far away home of the blest;" the fishes leap from the clear blue sea and are not afraid; the nightingale chants the sweet melodies. The garden is lighted by the moon and stars, the clouds are never dark, the sky never sad, the earth never unproductive, and the inhabitants are always lighthearted and glad ; there are no old, or ugly, or sick, or lame, or blind to be found in this garden—this Land of the Beautiful. The government is the best, and all the people are rich and good.

The people outside, ever look toward this garden

with envious, longing hearts ; they curse their own land—its meagerness and poverty ; they sigh for the richness and warmth of the beautiful garden. They go about their work with sullen and angry brows. The clouds hang over them, dark and heavy, or the sun is so hot and parching that they wish they might forget their existence, if they cannot get into this garden. They neglect to plant flowers and fruits ; they do not feed their birds, and they fly from their homes. When the rain falls they do not water their fields ; when the floods come they do not drain their lands, and so they have poor harvests. They have no beautiful homes to go to when "The day is done." They say, "Ours is a poverty-stricken land, and God has forsaken us—we have nothing to live for, let us die ;" and they grow old before the noonday, and great lines of care gather on their brows. They are poor, neglectful, unloving, and their life is merely existence. They have no hope, no bright dreams, no ambition. They say, "We are not of the blessed few, and there is no good in these things. If life has joys for us, they will come without our exertions, so—let us rest!" and they lie idle in the shade of the trees, too hope-less to dream, too envious to see the lovely tints in their own sky, or hear the sweet murmur of the waters, or note the beautiful verdure of their forest. They do not see that the dwellers in the Beautiful Valley are workers. They do not know that they are happy because they

> " Gather up the sunshine
>   Lying all along their path;
> And keep the wheat and. roses,
>   Casting out the thorns and chaff."

They do not notice that they take each rest as they journey life's road, and drink from each cooling fountain, and that if they see shadows lying in the valley around them, they look up and see sunshine gilding the tops of the mountains.

BURIED DREAMS.

> " Hark! A voice from the far-away;—
> ' Listen and learn,' it seems to say,
> ' All to-morrow shall be as to-day,
>   The cord is frayed, and the source is dry,
>   The link must break, and the lamp must die,
>   Good-bye, Hope, good-bye, good-bye!' "

Good-bye, Hope! Ah, no, we can never say good-bye, Hope. We cannot bid ● go away forever. We have listened and learned, and there comes this message from the ages that are past,—"Hope on, hope ever."

As I sit here, the shadows creep up from the misty gulf and lie thick around me. The scenes that were bright this morning grow faint and fainter. I can scarcely see the white cliff that rises just a little way down the beach, and yet it is quite as large as it was this morning; only the fogs of the evening envelop it now. And shall I think, because the lights are dim, that they will always remain so? Ah no! "Weeping may endure for a night, but joy cometh in the morning." And so, bright-winged Hope, be up and on your mission. Thick shadows lie all along our path, but there is always a clearing ahead.

We dream one bright dream—it fades, and dies, leaving only the ashes behind; but soon another comes; the brightness is renewed, the fire lighted again. Our hearts are miniature worlds. In the busy, active world, a great man, a genius, flashes up, kindles the universe with the enthusiastic praise of his powers, is lauded for his brief hour—then comes death, oblivion; he drops out of the grand system of mental planets, and is lost to the present, and the future knows him not. So with our hearts. One grand chain of thoughts, plans and ideas, fill them to-day; to-morrow they have vanished, and we take up new ones.

Sometimes these old dreams lie buried for years among the debris of driftwood, mouldering to ashes, and we heed them not, until some day a little incident, a leaf from an old book, a line from a letter, yellow with age, a bunch of withered flowers, a snatch from an old song, or the scent of a flower, recalls these dreams of long ago. We gather up the ashes, and perhaps find a faint spark of vitality, a feeble glow of warmth, and we live over again the "auld lang syne." We revel again in our young ambitions, recall the bright hopes that lent them color, and see our mansions in the air rising high as of yore, and yet—we know they are only dreams:

> "Alack! they are dead, and their grace has fled,
> Forever and evermore."

It may be that our thoughts wander back to the early days of our sweet love dreams. We recall the old school house, and the "one" for whom our heart beat fastest; and, for a moment, we wonder if we ever have loved any one else as well as that one, "first love."

Then we recall another dream which came later ; remember the sweet words which fell from other lips,

and we feel that this was our first real love; aye, we
let some tears fall as we close down the coffin lid on
these old dreams; for though years have passed, and
the old loves are married and scattered, yet, even yet,
they have power to stir the deep well of our affections. These dreams are the offspring of our heart
and brain, and we come across one as we travel along
the highways of life; it touches us, and we rebuke
ourselves for our fickleness and utter weakness of
purpose. We wonder how we could have put aside
all those heart-thrills; how we could have lived such
recklessly careless lives; and for one moment we believe that life's joys all lie behind us, that our hearts
can only find a ceaseless echo of pain, and we repeat
sadly :

> " I've done with all beneath the stars,
>   O world so vainly fleeting;
> How long against Time's ruthless bars
>   Have the soul's wings been beating!
> Till even the soul but yearns for sleep,
>   Calm rest, for fevered riot,
> The sacred sleep, the shadows deep
>   Of death's majestic quiet."

But thank God, these troubled dreams do not
come often, and they soon fly away and hide themselves again. They are our shadowy sorrows, and

come, like ghosts, in the twilight, and flee in the sunlight.

> " Perhaps from the loss of all we may learn
>   The song which the seraph sings—
> A grand and glorious psalm—
>   That will tremble and rise, and rise and thrill,
> And fill our breast with its grateful rest,
>   And its lonely yearnings still."

When the memory of these old dreams is stilled,
we come back to our Present. Yes, it is OURS—we
hold its joys in our grasp. The Past belongs to
Memory, to God, and the grave. The Present belongs
to us. The old dreams were sweet, but the dreams of
to-day are brighter—the living loves of to-day are
sweeter than the dead loves—the ghosts of the Past.

> " Sorrow is shadow to life, moving where life doth move,
>   Not to be laid aside, until we lay living aside."

If sorrow is shadow-life, joy is sunshine; they
are equal, and we will never be done with sunlight
and shadow until we glide into "That change which
never changes."

AN IDYL.

PART FIRST.

A maiden sat in the sunshine weaving a beautiful fabric in Fancy's golden loom—a fabric shot with silver and sprinkled with jewels, and as rich as ever enveloped the form of royalty in its costly folds. What she wove in imagination was a wondrous web of happiness, of good works, of noble achievements ; a web which God's hand must touch before human weaver could call it perfect. She was painting her future destiny on the swift movements of the shuttle as it shot from side to side, cutting the fabric into richest garments of hope, and love, and peace, and happiness. The roses blooming at her feet sent up their fragrance, as the light winds stirred their slumbrous leaves. But a stronger puff of the same winds tore the petals from their stems, and they lay scattered and withered at her feet.

A step came up the garden walk, and the dream fled away to be taken up at some other time. She looked shyly up—her lover stood at her side. Youthful dimples spread themselves over the sweet young face, and a happy light gleamed in the dreaming eyes.

The dreams of the future were forgotten in the bliss of the present, and the tender hopes, love's fruition, seemed fully present with her now.

The golden sunlight fades out, the stars come forth and twinkle faintly above, the night winds rustle the leaves over head, and carry the shattered roses away, leaving tender kisses on the two happy young faces. Low words of love and trust and hope, pass their lips; promises of fidelity and pledges of truth are whispered; a good-bye is spoken, a warm passionate kiss, a close embrace, and it is over. One goes out into the world, to "do and to dare," and the other remains in a nest of roses, to dream and to hope; and God is over all—yes, God is over all.

PART SECOND.

Silently the shadows creep up over the hill-tops, silently the days fly past, and are numbered with the things that were; aye, silently the days, and months, and years have past away. The great shuttle of Time has woven dark threads into the beautiful fabric; it is stained here and there with tears, the gold is tarnished, the jewels have dropped from their silver settings, and—the world goes on—Time goes on forever.

The shadows have deepened over the young life—
the smiles rarely come now, and yet she strives to be
gay—strives to still the wild throbbings of her aching
heart, working daily at the common-place duties of
life, trying to forget the pain of the past, and to close
her eyes against the blank, desolate future, trying
vainly to forget the days that once seemed brighter
than now—than they ever will again ; crushing back
her hopeless grief, and smiling even through a mist
of tears that will come, praying for a stronger will to
meet the ills of life. But the roses are crushed out,
their fragrance has died away, and nothing remains
to tell that they have been.

How hard it is to believe that "good most is ;"
how hard for anguished lips to say ʻ Thy will;" how
hard to believe that "There is but one great Right
and Good, and that Wrong and Ill are shades thereof,
and not substance." Sad hearts see no good in evil ;
breaking hearts feel no good in the loss of their idols;
strong hearts are hushed in the stillness of despair ; strong hands are still in their agony ; firm
lips grow pale with suffering; brave hearts falter
at the picture of future desolation, as they see the
twilight coming on ; brave souls murmur at the heavy
burden of their woe. And though the roses bloom

and fade and bud again in other years, their fragrance comes no more into their lives, and the shadows of twilight settle about them.

The maiden has grown into a woman, her sorrows have made her older than have the years; still, she sees no hidden beauty ahead, and her pale lips falter as she repeats :

" From all that live I live apart,
   An age has passed me in a day;
Its joys have ripened in my heart,
   Its cares have touched and left me gray."

She looks into the gathering gloom and sees no stars; she hears not the songs of the birds; the winds are not soft and caressing, but cold and cutting. She tries to repeat, "As Thou wilt," but cannot,—no, not yet. Still, God is over all.

PART THIRD.

The Autumn has come, the fruits are ripe and ready to gather, and the hilltops are gorgeous in their rich autumnal robe placed there by Nature's hand.

A woman with a sweet face and full of peace and love, full of grave tenderness and gentleness, looks out into the sunshine and smiles lovingly on the little children who greet her. She is glad of the beautiful day, of the sunshine and beauty of earth. The light falls in clear warm rays across her silvered hair. With her the joyousness of youth is past, the anguish of disappointment fled, the rebellion against life over, the heaviness of heart gone, and a deep, abiding peace fills her heart. She thinks tenderly over the "pleasures that will never come again," but the bitterness is past, and life has its WORK.

Her woman-life has found a deep meaning in the sorrows of her girlhood; she has meekly shouldered the burdens of life, and filled up many hours with blessed toil. She dreams no more, but works. The shuttle of Time is flying swiftly now, weaving in bright colors, not of thoughts, but of actions; filling up the fabric of human destiny with beautiful threads of goodness.

The maiden is a woman now—a true, brave worker; and the world is better for her living. The sorrows of youth have purified and ennobled her, and life has a broader meaning than self, and she says with true faith now, "If evil most seem, yet good most is."

> " Some plants must blossom in the light,
>   And some in shady places set,
> Must bear full many a change and blight,
>   Before perfection shall be met."

We know not what is best for us, but be sure that GOD IS OVER ALL..

EXTRACTS.

In accordance with the plan laid out in the beginning of man's supremacy on earth, the wicked are bound to suffer. Men may argue that there is no hell—no final and everlasting punishment; they may fill the world with mad theories and unhallowed faiths; may turn the doctrines or faith of our fathers —whom we were wont to believe were good men—upside down; may show that our mothers were " blind leaders of the blind," or weak superstitious women, who accepted implicitly the faith of their ancestors; may—as Bob Ingersol of our own day is doing—talk loudly of the foolhardiness of a faith which would, under any circumstances, launch one into perdition; may boldly announce that they have no respect for any one who believes in a hell—and who can bear to lose respect for so great and good a man as Bob Ingersol!—but believe as we may, the fact stands firm, and will not be uprooted to sprout new doctrine or new theories which are a weariness to the brain, and always are leading one a mad chase after Truth, until he grows misanthropic and distrustful of everything.

—[Lights and Shadows.

THE tides cannot stand still, any more than the wild surgings of the human brain; both are controlled by an invisible power—an impulse too strong to resist. We may struggle against a bitter thought until it is somewhat softened and modified, but another comes first, it may be gentler, sweeter, but it is only a prelude to another outburst of infinite misery, and the thralldom is even more complete than if it had been allowed to take its course at first—it has ripened and gathered new force. Men have been maddened—their intellects cramped into such circumscribed bounds that the stamp of idiocy was visible; by the overwhelming strength of a bitter thought. So it is with the tides—they rise slowly, gradually, but they gain force until their strength is resistless, overpowering ; and with the rise of the winds, ships are submerged, strewing the waters with the wrecks and the valuable cargo of human lives.

—[IBID.

BREAKING UP.

How much it means—how full of deep import! Breaking up! Scattering the dreams of a lifetime to the winds ; burying the hopes of long years of toil and privation in the deep river of Regret; letting loose the strong anchor of the ideal and beatific, and grasping—what? Only a few withered leaves. The apples have turned to ashes in the hand—the leaves have withered and faded. Every thing has proved a mockery.

Breaking up! The children you have toiled and prayed for—have planned and dreamed for—are not up to your ideal standard, and that is a cross heavy to bear. As the years have lengthened you have become reconciled to that. But this is hard—to toil so long, so patiently, so uncomplainingly, for them ; then when the shadows of age creep into the dear eyes which have watched them so patiently, the children must fly from the old nest—must try some other home. First goes the eldest—a daughter ; the child of many prayers. She finds strong arms to plead for her ; and, forgetful for awhile, she rushes away into the new, untried life, and leaves the father and mother to fight the remaining years without her. Cruel, is it? Who can tell? Nature has decreed it so, and we must not judge.

After the first break in the chain, the links seem easy to snap. Then follow the boys, one by one,—each going to win a future of his own; till now, out of the six, only one remains. One, the ewe lamb of the flock—the Isaac, the child of your old age. Gone! Drifted away from the sheltering care of the parents;

> " Drifting, drifting to lands unknown,
>   From a world of love and care;
> Drifting away to a home untried,
>   And hearts that are beating there;"

and yet they push out, heedless of the pain and heart-ache they are causing.

You are left alone now—settled down after hard toil and busy care for the children—to an old age of loneliness. You live now, not on dreams of the future, but on recollections of the past; recollections mixed with pain and joy, but beautiful to you, because they are of a time when the "little ones" were at home.

And slowly as the waves creep nearer your feet and the tide rises to bear you, who have loved us so,

out on its bosom to the beautiful Beyond, you will see
and know and feel that,

> " The seed must be buried deep in earth
>   Before the lily opens to the sky;
>   So 'light is sown,' and gladness has its blith
>   In the dark deeps where we can only cry.

> " 'Life out of death,' is Heaven's unwritten law;
>   Nay, it is written in a myriad forms;
>   The victor's palm grows on the fields of war,
>   And strength and beauty are the fruit of storms.

> " Come then, my soul, be brave to do and bear;
>   Thy life is bruised that it may be more sweet;
>   The cross will soon be left, the crown we'll wear—
>   Nay, we will cast it at the Savior's feet;

> " And up among the glories never told,
>   Sweeter than music of the marriage bell,
>   Our hands will strike the vibrant harp of gold
>   To the glad song, 'He doeth all things well.' "

THE END.